EDGE OF EXISTENCE

—·—

FRANKIE CAMERON

FUNNY FACE FICTION LTD.

DEDICATION

This book is dedicated to Maddox, Akita, Chilli, Max, George, Frosty and Sassy - the best fur babies ever.

CONTENTS

CHAPTER ONE

Sofia
April 27th, 2049

It wasn't the resounding crash that alerted Sofia Cutter to the Presidents' presence in the Oval Office, but the two secret service agents stationed outside the door. Standing statue still, the two muscle-bound agents wore dark suits with buttoned-up white shirts. Li Zheng and DeShawn Durant had been part of James' eight-person security team since his inauguration. Tall, fit with buzz cuts, spiral white communication devices poked out discreetly in their ears. James' assistant Stephan lowered his head and looked away, determined to avoid eye contact.

"Mrs. Cutter." Zheng shook her head slightly and made a face before opening the door. A warning of her husband's mood.

James sat at the resolute desk at the south end of the room. Turned towards the three windows that overlooked the green lawn, the sun streamed down on his face as he slumped in his chair. He didn't move. A smile graced his lips but not his eyes as Sofia entered. He looked as if he had the weight of the world on his shoulders. A broken vase lay smashed between the chairs in front of the fireplace. He would be in big trouble if he marked the neoclassical mantel. Built in 1909, it had already survived the 1929 White House fire.

Sofia avoided stepping on any of the broken fragments, but neither did she try to pick up the pieces. James could clean up his own mess or more than likely he would call someone to do that. Did the secret service do housework? Sofia made her way towards him, skirting the presidential seal embedded in the carpet.

"Do you feel better now, James?"

"Not even slightly." He played with the emerald tie he wore loosely around his neck while she approached. Worry lines framed his mouth, creases surrounded his deep brown eyes that were underlined with black smudges.

"What did that poor vase ever do to you?"

He waved away her question. "Don't fret, Sofia. I'll pick up my mess."

"Well, I hope that wasn't a Ming vase or something older than time. Did we sign a waiver when we moved in? Saying we aren't responsible for any damage we do while living here? Because we don't have money to waste on stupidity."

James chuckled, rubbing absently at his chin. "No, but maybe we should have. Typical lawyer, always worried about liability."

Sofia slipped off her high heels. Using the desk for balance, she cursed them. The devil must have designed high heels. They were only nine months into James' term, and Sofia was already sick of wearing them. She hated having to do her auburn hair every morning, wishing she could put it into a ponytail and slip into pajamas and slippers. Not your typical first lady, Sofia fulfilled the duties the best she could, but her heart wasn't up to the task.

James opened his arms, then tilted back his chair. Sofia climbed onto his lap, into his embrace. Pushing his salt and pepper hair back off his face, Sofia swore the gray had more than doubled since he had become President. The lines around his eyes were deeper too. Something had been bothering him lately, but he wouldn't say what. Every time she asked, he changed the subject.

"Do you want to talk about it? Or can you?" Sofia rested her head against his chest, listening to the familiar thump of his beating heart. The President had little time to snuggle anymore. These moments alone were preciously few.

At 44, Joseph James Slade Cutter was the third youngest President in history behind Roosevelt and Kennedy. Alabama-born; he still had his heavy southern accent. His accent was one of the things that attracted Sofia, a New York City girl, to him initially in college. One governorship and twin seventeen-year-old sons later, he was still as attractive as the first time she met him.

"I can't. I want to, but I can't." He sighed again and scrubbed his hand over his face.

"Let me guess. It's a matter of National Security. You have been claiming that a lot lately. I wish I knew how to help you." Sofia originally thought this would have been more of a partnership. Graduating at the top of her class from Harvard Law School, she had practiced at a prestigious law firm before James began his presidential run. Sofia expected to be more than just a decoration.

"You do enough already. I know this... life isn't—."

"What I wanted."

He nodded.

"It isn't, but you are." Sofia felt a hollowness in her chest that somehow still felt heavy. Her depression was getting worse, no matter how she tried to combat it. She had tried meditation, medication, yoga and many other things, but she couldn't seem to shake the darkness. Some days it was all she could do to get out of bed.

"Am I? I hope so, because I need you. The boys need you."

"Don't say the United States needs me or I will suffocate you in your sleep with a pillow." Sofia jabbed him in the chest with her finger.

James threw back his head and laughed. "There's the old Sofia. I haven't seen her in a while."

Sofia's watch beeped, and she groaned. Unwrapping herself from James' embrace, she rose, mentally bracing herself for the next scheduled appointment. Another boring luncheon to endure. Another rah-rah speech to give. Different from arguing in front of the Supreme Court for first amendment rights like she did in the past.

"Try not to annihilate anyone verbally this afternoon." James stood and kissed her on top of the head.

It had been a while since she had done that. "No promises." Sofia noticed a stain on her pink chiffon dress, now she would have to change. She checked her watch again. "What's on your agenda this afternoon."

"Oh, you know... just saving the world." James gave a half shrug.

"Is that all. Well then, just don't be late for dinner."

"Speaking of which, the boys are coming this weekend, correct?"

Her boys were her favorite subjects. Joe and Rob, identical twins. Joe was a quiet healer, a volunteer with the ambulance services. He was happier alone than with other people. In the fall, he was off to start his undergrad education on the road to becoming a doctor.

Rob was a ball of energy, never stopping. He had ambitions of becoming a firefighter. Sofia and James had talked him into getting his fire science degree first, putting off the inevitable, knowing that he would rush into danger every time he had a chance. He loved the feel of adrenaline in his veins. Rob liked to be the center of attention, surrounded by people just like his father.

The boys hadn't wanted to leave their last year of high school in Montgomery, Alabama, so they stayed behind when James and Sofia moved to Washington. Sofia's widowed mother Lenore had moved into their home to stay with them. Sofia transitioned back and forth as often as she could, but too often, she felt pulled in both directions and felt like a failure.

"Joe is, but Rob has a girl he wants to take out on Friday night. His secret service—."

"No, Rob needs to come to Washington. Your mother too." James spoke in a voice usually reserved for his staff.

"Excuse me." His tone didn't impress Sofia, and she let him know it. He might be important to the world, but Sofia still ran the family. "Well, can't he come next weekend instead? I think it is spring formal."

"No, have the secret service drag him here if they have to, but I need them both here this weekend. It's not negotiable."

Sofia looked at him curiously. He wasn't acting like himself. Normally, he had nerves of steel, but now he seemed anxious. Lately, he had taken to having nightmares, twisting and turning all night, waking up covered in sweat as if he had fought a battle.

Sofia waited for him to explain further, but he remained silent. She pivoted to leave the room just before Susie Wang, James' petite chief of staff, bounced in, her short dark bob swaying back and forth.

Susie seemed surprised to see Sofia. Her eyes widened at Sofia's shoeless feet, but she didn't comment. They exchanged pleasantries.

Sofia reached down to pick up her shoes. Before she reached the door, James spoke.

"Sofia... tell Rob he can come here Saturday."

Sofia nodded without turning around. Her angry image reflected from the long-case clock as she exited from the northeast door.

The President's family dining room was much smaller than the state dining room it was located beside. A long mahogany table that seated twelve took most of the space in the room. A parquet floor peeked out from underneath the muted tan area rug. Fine china and fancy drinking glasses rested on the table, covered with a long red tablecloth. A matching side table held two crystal candle holders in the shape of a swan with long white tapers. French doors led to a small private garden. Sofia pulled down the blinds to hide the secret service agents parked outside the door.

Sofia dismissed the White House staff after they brought in the food, hoping for an intimate family meal. The chef had surpassed herself in preparing the boys' favorite foods. They loved southern cooking, including BBQ pulled pork, shrimp, country fried steak, fried chicken, fried dill pickles and fried green tomatoes. They would eat fried anything. The boys, younger versions of their father, loved southern food.

Lenore, Sofia's mother, picked through the food on her plate, less than impressed. "Fried cooking, don't you think I get enough of this... food, living in that god-forsaken state? Couldn't we have had prime rib or a steak?" Lenore tucked her hand through her curly, short grey locks.

"Grandma, Alabama and god-forsaken don't belong in the same sentence." Joe pushed back his shoulder-length dirty blond hair from his face. Joseph James Slade Cutter, the third, preferred to be called Joe.

"G'ma, southern cooking is the best." Rob stabbed his fork into another piece of chicken, plopping it onto his plate.

Rob kept his hair clipped short, military style. Even if they were bald, Sofia could tell them apart from their mannerisms something as simple as the way they turned their heads. It was easier for others now that Rob had a jagged white scar that ran along the bottom of his chin. The result of the combination of a bike, a ramp, and a poor decision.

"Rob, how many times have I told you not to call me that? I am not a rapper." Lenore curled her lips.

The conversation was light while Rob and Joe discussed their future. James seemed distracted, only listening half-heartedly and not adding much to the conversation.

"What do you think, Dad?" Joe bit into a pickle. His first plate of food was almost gone.

"Gees, I wish I could eat like you, Joe, bottomless pit for a stomach and gain no weight." Sofia teased.

"Hmm, I'm sorry, Joe, can you repeat that? I am afraid I drifted off." James scratched the side of his neck. His body was present, but his mind was somewhere else.

"I was asking what med school you thought I should attend. Everyone always talks about Harvard, but I'm thinking John Hopkins."

"Who turns down Harvard?" Rob said. "Mom went there."

Rob winked at Sofia. His favorite thing to do was annoy his brother. If Joe pumped gas, then Rob would lock him out of the car; if Joe walked up the stairs, Rob would try to trip him or swat him in the butt; if Joe said black, Rob said white just to irritate his older brother by sixteen minutes.

"Don't look at me like that," Joe said.

"Like what? I can't help what my face does when you speak."

"Remember when I asked for your opinion? Yeah, me neither. I'm interested in dad's opinion, not yours." Joe crushed his napkin in his hand. "Dad?"

"Sofia, aren't you going to say something to your boys?" Lenore tapped her perfectly painted watermelon-colored nails against the table. "You let them away with too much."

"Boys, please," Sofia bristled against the criticism. She could never make her mother happy. "That better mom?"

"You aren't going to medical school, so it doesn't matter." James pushed back his chair, rising to his feet.

"What, of course he is James, they have already accepted him everywhere he applied." Sofia exchanged puzzled looks with the boys. "Why would you say that?"

James shoved his hands through his hair, pacing back and forth. He stopped to say something, shook his head, then started pacing again. Finally stopping, he grabbed the top of the chair, leaning on it, his knuckles turned white from the pressure.

"What I am about to tell you is top secret. This information cannot be told to anyone else. No one, not your classmates, not even your secret service. Absolutely no one else. It doesn't leave this room, EVER."

He had a captive audience. Sofia's stomach clenched after she met James' worried gaze and saw the fear in his eyes. She knew James well enough to know this terrified him.

"James, what is it? You're scaring me. Whatever you have to say can't be that bad." Sofia put her hand on her chest, feeling it beat faster. She rose from her chair, but he motioned for her to stay seated.

"Don't worry, we never talk about you, dad. Bringing you up is a buzz kill." Rob stuffed another fried dill pickle in his mouth.

"Never. Not even when you were governor. Contrary to popular opinion, it doesn't make us more popular. It's worse now that the secret service follows us everywhere we go." Joe rolled his eyes.

"Will you please just stop talking and listen?" He slammed his hand down on the table with a bang. "This is a big secret that you will have to keep for two months. You are going to want to tell people. But you can't. in fact, this might be the hardest thing you ever do."

"Will you just get to the point? Spit it out already." Lenore threw her napkin down over her half-eaten plate.

"NASA has tracked a large near-earth object on a collision course with Earth. Two months from now, an asteroid named Attila will strike. Life as we know it is about to change." James met Sofia's gaze, and she saw the fear in his eyes.

Sofia's thoughts ran wildly. What did they mean for her boys, her mother, for them? She ran her tongue over her lips. Her mouth had lost all its moisture. "Wh... what are you saying?"

"Ah, there must be a plan right." Joe's eyes narrowed. "You are going to do something, right?"

"Are we sending oil drillers to blast it?" Rob asked.

"This isn't the movie Armageddon, Rob." Joe said. "We are not sending people into space to drill."

"I wish it was that easy, but that is fiction, and this is reality." A bead of sweat broke out on James' lip.

"What...," Sofia couldn't corral her thoughts. This couldn't be real. Her anxiety had her in its grip. She couldn't think, she couldn't move. She couldn't take her eyes off her boy's faces. Fear clutched her heart and made thinking impossible.

"James, if this is a joke, I, for one, am not impressed." Lenore shoved her chair away from the table and stood. "Now, if you'll excuse me, it has been a long day."

"STAY where you are. Now all of you listen to me and zip your lips." James spoke through clenched teeth.

"Two years ago, my predecessor sent a mission to examine the composition of the asteroid. I won't bore you with the details, but the asteroid is indestructible. It should have skirted the earth by miles, like Apophis in 2029, but an in-space collision with another mass object changed its trajectory four years ago. It is unavoidable, it will hit Earth and the result will be catastrophic."

"What will happen to us?" Sofia asked.

"I don't know yet." James answered, his expression devoid of any hope.

CHAPTER TWO

Terra
April 27th, 2049

The blinker clicked, Terra checked the side mirror, spotting another convoy of enormous green military trucks rolling down the street. By the looks of the caravan, she wouldn't be going anywhere for a while. Turning off the ignition, she hunted through her car, looking for a stick of gum. The taste of grape exploded in her mouth.

What was going on at the military base? There was a lot more activity up there than usual. Was President Cutter scheduled for a visit? Colorado Springs was busier than it had been for years.

Terra tapped her hands on the steering wheel to the beat of the music. She kept looking for an end to the procession, or at least a red light.

The buzzing of her cell phone caught Terra's attention. She debated answering, but it was her older sister who would only call back insistently until Terra picked up. "Hey, Tess."

"Hi. Where are you? What's that noise?" Tess asked.

"Stuck outside the grocery store waiting for a convoy to pass." Terra rolled up the window to cut the noise from the street and the dust from the big trucks. The green 1970 Monte Carlo she drove didn't have automatic windows. Her sister thought she was nuts for driving this old car, but there was something stylish about the machine. Plus, Terra loved the sound of the engine and how fast the V-8 picked up speed. It guzzled gas like a drunken sailor, but she loved it anyway.

"I keep telling you to park in the lot, not the street. Who parallel parks anymore? You know we have self-parking cars now, right?"

"Yeah, yeah, yeah." Terra checked the mirror again. This was worse than waiting for a train at a crossing. "So, are we still going to the movies tonight?"

"Can't. Just got dragged into work. That's why I called. Two nurses on my floor are down with the flu and I can't turn down the overtime."

Terra popped a bubble. "Ok, no problem. We can go another night."

Terra's family all had medical degrees. Her father was an oncologist, while her mother was a psychiatrist. It pleased neither of them when Terra received an undergraduate in English with a minor in journalism. Medicine just didn't interest her. Her parents were both gone now, killed in a car accident four years ago on the way to her high school graduation. Tess was her only remaining family.

"I'll check the schedule when I get to the hospital and get back to you. K love ya, bye."

Terra tossed the phone onto the console as the last truck rumbled by, allowing her to pull the car out into the street. With no plans now for the evening, she debated what to do with the rest of her day. When the convoy turned right, Terra did the same. Staying far enough back that it didn't look like she was following. Her journalist instincts were itching.

The trucks swung onto I-25, exiting on state highway 115, before turning onto NORAD road, government property. At the entrance to the Cheyenne Mountain Complex, the trucks waited in a long line to get checked by security before entering.

There was no getting past the 12-foot fence and barbed wire, not to mention the guards with guns. Terra wondered where she could get a closer look. Deciding to backtrack to the split in the road, she took the fork to the left. At the end of a dead-end road, she pulled over and opened the trunk, then sorted through the contents until she found binoculars. At the last minute, Terra grabbed a bottle of water, then stuffed her iPhone in her back pocket.

After hiking up the hill, Terra followed along the fence line, looking for a weak point. She looped the binoculars over her neck. There was nothing in sight but trees and rocks. Terra debated leaving, but then decided to search for a few minutes longer. The sun was still high enough in the sky that there would be light for a few more hours. She watched the sky for drones, helicopters, or any type of security.

The fence had stood in the hills since the 1960s, becoming part of the landscape. Trees had grown around and through the barricade. When she approached the top of the second elevation, she noticed a tree had fallen through the fence, slicing a rip in the netting. It wasn't large, but it might be big enough for Terra to slip through.

Terra removed her jacket and binoculars, then pushed them through to the other side. She tucked the water bottle into the front pocket of her sweatshirt. Taking the elastic from her wrist, she twisted her long, dark hair into a messy bun.

With her hands, she scooped dirt, trying to enlarge the hole. Terra pushed the wire netting as wide as it would go. When she thought it was wide enough, Terra dropped her head and began wiggling through to the other side; headfirst, backside up.

The plan worked well until her jeans caught on something, trapping her under the fence. Terra tried to reverse, but couldn't. She reached for the phone in her back pocket, but one hand was trapped beneath her in the dirt while the other hand couldn't quite stretch that far. She entwined her free hand around the clops of dirt, pulling with all her strength, but she didn't move. She closed her eyes and took a deep breath to calm herself.

What was she doing? Why was she even here? Why did she always let her curiosity get the best of her? Nobody even knew where she was. Panic set in. She pulled and pushed, cursed and swore and wiggled until finally, she was free. Free and on the military side of the fence.

Standing, Terra leaned over and brushed off the dirt before she heard a gun click. Looking up, her eyes fixated on the barrel of a military rifle.

"Hands up." A rough voice spoke.

Terra lifted her hands in surrender. Her heart thudded so loudly in her ears that it was all she could hear. Raising her eyes to the soldier holding the gun, she discovered the biggest blue eyes she had ever seen.

Terra swallowed hard, afraid to move or to give an explanation. What statement could she give when he caught her in the act? What was the punishment for sneaking into a military base? Would she go to military jail or regular jail? She couldn't stop the questions in her brain from multiplying.

"You are trespassing on government property." The soldier kept his rifle trained on Terra. Dressed in military fatigues, his hat sat backward on his head, a few strands of dark brown hair poked out from underneath. His oval face was deadly serious in contrast to his soft blue eyes. "It is illegal for you to be here according to Section 1282 of title 18."

"I'm sorry... Sergeant... Edge, is it?" Terra checked the white lettering on his pocket for his name while she tried to produce a better explanation than curiosity. He seemed young, maybe in his early twenties, her age; tall, fit and clean shaved a few inches over six feet.

"Private." He lowered his rifle to the side and clicked on the safety.

"Excuse me?"

"Private Edge, not Sergeant." He pointed to the insignia attached to his uniform.

"Oh, right?" Terra had noticed that he only had one stripe instead of three. Living close to a military base, it was impossible not to recognize ranks and insignias.

"As if you didn't know the difference. Flattery doesn't work on me."

Terra shrugged, feigning an innocent impression.

"Do you have Identification?"

"Not on me, but I have my phone, and my entire life is in it. There must be some... identification on it." How much longer would she have to stand here, hands raised? Her arms were aching from their unnatural position.

"Where?"

"My back pocket."

With his weapon still up, he clicked on the safety, then draped the rifle over his shoulder. He stepped so close Terra could hear him breathe, then he reached around her to pull the phone from her back pocket. His touch was gentle but firm as she felt the phone move. He stepped away. "You can put your arms down now, but don't try... anything."

Terra shook out her arms.

"Passcode?" The soldier looked down at the phone.

"8771"

He punched in the numbers, then thumbed through some screens and handed her back the phone. "Terra Baxter. Twenty-one, Caucasian, green eyes, pert nose, mahogany brown hair, five feet three inches."

"That's not all on my phone, is it?" Terra's eyebrows squished together.

"No, but I have eyes."

A radio crackled with a voice asking for an update. The private walked a few steps away to answer the call, turning his body away so she couldn't overhear his conversation. Terra didn't move until he returned, except for shuffling her feet in the dirt. Were they coming to arrest her?

Before he returned, Private Edge swung the rifle around until it hung behind his back. "I didn't report you, but if I ever see you here again, I'll have no choice. I'll have to arrest you. You are free to leave."

"How?"

"The same way you came in, crawl out of the hole." He waved his hand at the fence, then took his hat off and replace it on his head properly. "I just reported the break in the fence, so someone will come to repair it. If you had cut the fence, this conversation would be entirely different."

Terra ran her tongue over her lips to moisten them. "Thank you." She graced him with a smile.

He paused, blinked, then turned his back and walked away. "Nice to meet you, Ms. Baxter."

Picking up the water bottle, Terra opened it and guzzled water, wiping her hand across her face. She plucked the binoculars from the ground, then shoved them back through the fence. Before she could stop herself, she yelled. "Hey, do you think you could help me?"

He turned around, paused, then stomped over to the fence. "What do you need?" The tone of his voice showed his level of displeasure. He secured his rifle against the fence.

"Could you just make sure I don't get stuck? Maybe bend the fence a little."

He crouched, wound his fingers into the bottom of the fence and bent the edge upward. He muttered, "I can't believe I'm doing this."

It seemed awkward to slither under the fence with him standing there watching her. Once again Terra went headfirst, but this time, backside down. She didn't want to be caught with her butt raised in the air, with the soldier staring at her. The few minutes it took to get back under felt like hours.

He chuckled roughly, "At what point did you think this was a good idea?"

Terra made it through the other side of the fence without issue, dusting off her pants. She promptly stood up to find him staring at her. "What?" She felt a little braver on this side of the fence. Terra picked up the binoculars and her water bottle.

He smiled slowly as if his face wasn't used to it. "What are you even doing up here? What were you trying to accomplish?"

"I just got lost hiking."

"So you deliberately crawled under a barbed wire fence. Try again. The info on your phone tells me you are a local. You know better."

Terra drew a pattern in the dirt with her foot while she contemplated what to tell him. "What does it matter?"

"Just curious."

"I could tell you, but then I'd have to kill you."

"I think that's my line. Cut the crap." His military scowl was back in place. His eyes flickered with impatience.

"What are you going to do? By the time you create a big enough hole to crawl under the fence, I'll be halfway back to Colorado Springs." Terra couldn't explain why she felt the need to tease this stern soldier.

"To where? 35 Valleyview drive?" He raised an eyebrow.

Damn, the iPhone gave away all her secrets. She wondered if the soldier had a good memory.

Terra's hair whipped across her face as a four-blade military camouflage green helicopter appeared over the horizon. It might have been a black hawk, but she wasn't sure. The whirl of the blades stirred up the dirt and scrub grass, bending the trees backward, and blowing everything around like a small cyclone. Terra shielded her face to stop the debris from blowing into her eyes.

Private Edge signalled to the helicopter that all was okay, and it flew away as quickly as it arrived. He tugged his hat lower on his head.

Undoing her ponytail, Terra ran her fingers through her hair, trying to untangle the mess her hair had become.

"I have to get back to work. Can I call you sometime?" He asked. Their eyes met briefly before he broke it off.

Where had that come from? Okay, maybe Terra had been flirting with him a little, but he was kind of cute when he smiled.

"Sure my number is—."

"719-797-2107" He tapped his index finger on the side of his head as he strode away.

CHAPTER THREE

Sofia
May 27, 2049

The delay at the gate was briefer than expected. The bomb dogs sniffed around their SUV while soldiers inspected the car with mirrors on long poles. Zheng and Durant exited the vehicle so the soldiers could perform a security scan. Standard military procedure at the Cheyenne Mountain Complex, even for the President and First Lady.

The boys and Lenore followed in the vehicle behind, along with their two dogs and three cats. Sofia threatened to remain behind if she couldn't take her fur babies. It was a deal breaker, and James knew her well enough to know that. Every time she thought about the people, the animals and everything left behind, her stomach clenched and her mind started spinning.

The arched opening that jutted from the imposing mountain looked ominous. Sad even, as if it knew the future. The military convoy drove right into the facility, through the massive tunnels. One tunnel bent sideways at a 90-degree angle. Sofia couldn't believe her eyes. It seemed like they had hollowed out the entire inside of the mountain.

James was speaking with Susie Wang, who prattled on about the facility. "Did you know miners excavated 693,000 tons of granite using more than a million pounds of explosives to hollow out the mountain in the 1960s? There are seven million cubic feet of hollowed-out space, almost four and a half acres of living space. Do you think that will be enough, Mr. President?"

James scrubbed his hand over his face. "No... but it will have to do."

"Enough... It's not near enough space. What does this bunker hold... 800 people maybe... only the top minds in the country are being saved...?" Sofia broke off and bit her lip, returning to staring out the window in silence.

"Sofia,—,"

"I know what you are going to say, James, but if this bunker holds 800 people, then we should fill it to capacity. Your plan to under-fill the bunker is ridiculous."

"Sofia, we have been through this more than enough times already." James' eyes flashed with irritation. He stacked the folders he had been thumbing through in a disorderly pile on the black leather seats. "We could be down here for decades. We can't risk extra people if we don't have the resources to feed and support them."

"Not good enough. We have to figure something out. Save everyone we can."

"I can't go through this with you again. I don't know what you think I can do. I'm just one... I'm doing the best I can with what I have to work with. Don't you think if I could do more I would?" James exhaled harshly, shook his head and turned away.

Sofia felt horrible. She wasn't angry with him; she wasn't even angry, just frustrated at being so helpless. If she wasn't the First Lady, she wouldn't be on the list. Why was her life more important than anyone else's? The simple answer: It wasn't. Survivor's guilt on top of her depression was killing her.

As soon as they stepped out of the vehicle, soldiers and lackeys surrounded James, handing him more manila folders filled with reports. Sofia's nose wrinkled from the damp smell of the tunnel. She guessed she would have to get used to it. The words flew at James so fast that Sofia could barely keep up.

"NORAD reports the asteroid is still on target. It should impact on..."

"The seeds from the Svalbard Global Seed Vault have arrived..."

"They set up the food plant..."

"The diesel-filled lake is at capacity 510,000 gallons..."

"The four lakes are full...."

"Workers are tightening the bolts as we speak. There are over 115,000 rock bolts hammered into granite so it may take a while..."

James gathered the reports without looking at them, then passed them to Susie.

"The geological fault has been further reinforced..."

"We stockpiled the extra equipment in the wal-marts..."

"Are there any reports from the other bunkers?" James asked.

A van pulled up, and men unloaded statues and art. Sofia overheard one man tell the other to take it easy, that they were unloading the Mona Lisa. "Why is the Mona Lisa here? Doesn't it belong to France?"

James didn't seem to hear her question.

Susie juggled her armload of folders. "Yes, but it was on loan to the New York Met, so the French government asked us to look after it. They think it will be safer here."

"Oh," Sofia couldn't figure out anything else to say. She felt stupid and out of place.

"Yes, the Raven Rock Mountain Complex and the Mount Weather Emergency Operations Center are ready to lock down..."

"Contractors are trying to expand the bunker, but they don't think there will be enough time. They discovered a hot spring..."

"We have eight truckloads of MREs moving into storage."

"The Vice President has moved into the Deep Underground Command Center..."

"The Secretary of Defense, as the designated survivor, will stay at the White House until..."

Zheng escorted Sofia out of the way. She waited until the boys and her mother pulled up. All this data was making her head spin. She concentrated on trying to get right with the fact that she was moving into an underground bunker for their safety. She couldn't focus on all the people she was leaving behind, her friends, her cousins, and her co-workers. If she thought about them, she would crumple into a ball and cry forever.

Captain Campbell walked up and introduced himself, interrupting her pity party. A tall man with a dark brown complexion and thickly lashed eyes, the captain would be their escort through the building to their accommodations. He described the residences as Sofia and her family walked with him. "The Navy constructed these fifteen buildings from battleship steel. They set them on 1,300 springs that weigh 1000 pounds each."

"That's crazy," Joe said. He carried his guitar on his back while he toted some of his prized possession in his two bags.

There were limits to how much they could bring inside the facility. Two bags to pack everything important a person owned in the world. Sofia gave her head a shake. The soldier only had one "go" or "button up" bag each. It was beyond selfish to worry about possessions when the world was ending.

"This whole thing is crazy," Rob said. Both boys had withdrawn over the course of these last two months, as if the secret they carried was too heavy to bear. "This is like Call of Duty."

"No need to play Fortnite or Counter Strike anymore, right? We're living in the game." Joe adjusted his guitar so it would quit smashing into his back as he walked.

Lenore walked in a stunned silence content with her own thoughts. Two young handsome soldiers carried her belongings while two others carried the pet crates. Did Private Edge and Smith know the world was ending?

They moved through security while the officers checked everything they brought in. Sofia removed her shoes and then tiptoed into a body scanner, the same type they used at the airports. If only they were just going on a trip.

A series of hallways and ramps interconnected the buildings. Captain Campbell pointed out that the trim color was different to distinguish the areas, but it all looked the same to Sofia. Maybe they would have a map to help them navigate.

The captain opened their accommodations, then he left to allow them time to settle in. After a quick inspection, Sofia seemed impressed with their quarters. Dining room, living room, four bedrooms and two bathrooms. It was much more than she expected.

The captain had explained that the lodgings ranged from compact rooms to small houses to dormitories, depending on your rank. He explained they had the best quarters available.

Sofia looked around the room that would be their home until the planet became habitable again or they died, whatever came first.

"Morning," James said when he finally woke late the next morning, rubbing the sleep out of his bruised eyes that mirrored his exhaustion. The circles grew darker every day. "Is there any coffee?"

"Yes, I just made some." Sofia's heart went out to him. No other U.S. President had ever faced a crisis like this one.

Chester, their cat, rubbed up against James' leg, purring. The other cats had gone into hiding and only came out to eat.

James hadn't come to bed until the wee hours of the morning. He ran a hand through his dishevelled hair. Pouring himself a cup, he sipped it, holding it in his hands for warmth.

Lenore and Sofia watched TV on the couch. One of Lenore's soap operas. Sofia thumbed through a magazine, restless. There must be something productive she could do. She didn't plan on spending her time down here on the couch.

She couldn't believe that Cypresses from Vincent van Gogh was hanging over her couch like it was a vacation photo or a regular painting. The government had tried to save all the art they could, hanging masterpieces all over the complex.

Rob and Joe strolled in with the dogs, with their customary level of noise, leaving their military escort outside the door. Kicking off their shoes on the welcome mat.

Sofia got up to fill the dog's water dish and feed them.

"Nice Homer Simpson pajamas, dad," Joe said.

"Nothing says survival like the Simpsons," Rob said. "Hey, guess who just joined the fire department? Start training tomorrow."

"Fire department?" Lenore couldn't keep the disbelief out of her voice. "There is a fire department here?"

"You hungry?" Sofia asked.

"I could eat," Joe said.

"I'm starving, mom. But can you actually cook... like actual food?" Rob teased.

"Yeah, I thought you just ordered food," Joe tilted his head to the side.

Sofia was a lot of things, but a cook was not one of them. "Ha ha boys. You should have been comedians. I can cook." Their apartment had a compact fridge, a hot plate, and a small cupboard. They would be expected to take their meals in the cafeteria with the others.

The boys looked at Sofia with disbelief.

"Well, I can make sandwiches. That's cooking. Right? Cereal, toast. The list goes on and on." Sofia washed her hands, then picked food from the fridge. She used more pressure than necessary to cut up the vegetables. Taking out her frustrations on the carrots and celery.

Joe said. "This place is wild. Did you know that there are four lakes inside the complex?"

"Five if you count the lake of diesel fuel," Rob added. He pulled a gallon of milk out of the fridge and poured a glass, gulped it down, then poured another.

"We didn't see them today, but Sergeant Singh, our escort, said maybe tomorrow. Singh said once we button-up we can go wherever we want without an escort. You should have seen Rob flirting with her, embarrassing." Joe yanked out another glass for his brother to fill. "Don't hog all the milk. Who knows when we'll get to drink it again?"

"Button up?" Lenore asked.

"He means once they lock us inside before the asteroid hits," James explained.

"If we survive you mean." Lenore muttered under her breath then turned up the volume of her TV program.

"The Sergeant took us to see the blast doors. They are ... at least three-feet thick and weigh twenty-five tons. You have to see them, Mom," Rob's voice held a tinge of excitement.

"Singh said the last time the doors closed for anything other than testing was on 9/11." Joe hauled a chair to the kitchen table. "It only takes forty-five seconds or something like that to close the door."

Sofia regarded her sons warily. Were they settling in or was it just a front? Every time she thought about the asteroid, it felt as if someone squeezed her heart. What if all these precautions weren't enough? What if her boys weren't safe here? Her boys had barely lived. Sofia always knew she would die someday but knowing the date it could happen was a terrible burden to bear.

"I was going to mention the fire department, boys, once we got settled in." James tried to steal a slice of tomato, but Sofia swatted his hand away.

"Yeah, we saw them practicing rappelling today. They train every day. There is a gym where they work out." Rob said. "You guys should see the tunnels in this place... they are massive... 40 feet wide and at least three stories high."

James cocked an eyebrow. "I've seen the entire facility. You know who I am, right?"

Rob pushed his father's shoulder playfully, then straddled a chair backward.

"Are you still President when the United States is half gone?" Lenore asked.

"I'm joining the fire department, too." Joe said. "Don't look so surprised, mom. The fire department does all the first aid in the facility. Plus, there will be doctors here, so maybe they can teach me things."

"I'm not surprised," Sofia snapped her lips together when she noticed she was standing with her mouth open.

"Tell that to your face," Joe replied.

"Hush, I'm sorry, it won't be med school but—." Sofia gathered some buns and lunch meat, arranging them on a platter.

"Why bother?" Lenore asked from her spot on the couch. She clutched the blanket, wrapping it around her tighter. "Is there any way to turn up the heat in here? I'm freezing?"

"That is so great boys, both of you. I am so proud of you for making the best out of this situation." Sofia ignored her mother's complaints. Her boys were making the best out of this bad situation. She needed to do the same.

"What are you going to do with your time down here, mom?" Rob asked.

"I don't know yet, but something," Sofia answered. "There must be something a Harvard-educated lawyer can do."

"You should have been a doctor. I told you that." Lenore said. "But oh no, you wanted to be a lawyer. What good is that here? There are no lawsuits to file."

Sofia slipped with the knife, almost jabbing at herself. How could she spend every day with her mother in close quarters with no privacy? It would take the patience of a Saint.

"I'm still cold. Can you turn up the heat, James?"

"Sorry Lenore, the natural temperature of the cave is around 55 degrees. The heat from the computer systems keeps the buildings around 72 degrees. If you are cold. I suggest you put on more clothing." James explained.

"How long are we going to stay down here, Dad? Do they know yet?" Joe asked. His hair had fallen across his face, making him look younger than seventeen.

"Can we go outside again? Just to breathe fresh air... just one more time before it happens." Rob leaned forward, rubbing his hands together.

"Do we really need to stay down here now, James? The asteroid won't strike for another month." Sofia, like Rob, wanted to spend as much time outside as possible until it was too late.

"No, it's protocol. Once you are inside, you can't leave again. I won't risk any of you being trapped outside when Attila arrives."

A knock sounded at the door a moment before Suzie Wong barged in. "Good morning, everyone. How are we today?"

James took it as his cue to leave the room to get dressed. He held up a finger to Susie to let her know he would be ready in a moment.

Her happy, bouncy spirit was too much for Sofia to deal with on top of her mother. "Susie, it is customary to wait until you hear the words 'come in' before you enter a room." Sofia waved the knife as she spoke. The muscles at the back of her neck tightened. "You can wait outside for James."

Susie looked crestfallen but left without comment. Sofia regretted hurting her feelings the minute the words came out of her mouth.

"Mom, that was mean." Joe shook his head as Rob dissolved into a fit of laughter. Burying his face in the crook of his arm to suppress the noise.

"Boys, I promise you, we'll get outside at least one more time before Attila arrives." Sofia could already feel the walls closing in. Even the COVID-19 quarantine didn't even feel this claustrophobic.

CHAPTER FOUR

Terra
May 27, 2049

Terra waited outside the restaurant, snapping her bubble gum. He was late again. She warned him last time that it would be the last time she waited, but here she was waiting again, and blowing bubbles. The wind was picking up, and it looked like rain. Terra scolded herself for forgetting an umbrella in her haste to get here on time.

Dressed in her finest, Terra paced back and forth in front of Mackenzie's Chop Shop on Tejon street. It was Colorado Springs finest steak house. She would do anything to avoid this dinner. He wanted to take her home to El Paso, Texas, for a weekend, to meet his parents, but she wasn't ready for that. Not after a few weeks of dating. But with his parents coming to town for his 24th birthday, he arranged this dinner. He didn't play fair, knowing that she wouldn't deny his birthday request.

So here she stood under the awning, waiting for the skies to open up. The dark clouds and thunder matched her mood. She felt butterflies flip around in her stomach. Her hand kept touching her hair, making sure that the expensive up-do she paid for was still holding, not that it would matter if it rained.

Two powerful arms grabbed Terra, lifting her in the air and spinning her around. Her dress billowed outward, almost exposing her underwear. She squealed, "Put me down, Devan."

"That's Private Edge to you. Wow, you look so pretty. When I saw you standing there, you almost took my breath away." Devan twirled her around so Terra could look into his eyes. He kissed Terra lightly before placing her back on her feet and drawing her close. Sticking his nose in her hair, he inhaled deeply. "God, you smell good, like rainbows and sunshine."

True to his word, Devan had called Terra the day after their encounter on the base. They had spent almost every moment together since whenever he could get off base. Unfortunately, plans with a soldier were written in pencil, never in pen because plans were always changing.

Terra had a flexible schedule since she worked as a freelance writer, writing newspaper articles and SEO blogs for small businesses. As long as she met her client's deadlines, it was up to her when she worked. She dreamed that someday she would have a job at the New York Times breaking big stories, but as a recent college grad, she had to start somewhere.

Devan the soldier was sombre, robotic and cheerless. Devan the man was fun, romantic and kind. It hadn't taken Terra long to fall for his charms once she got to know him.

"Are you ready?" he asked.

"Not even slightly. Remind me why we are doing this again." Terra smoothed Devan's tie. She had never seen him in a suit before, and it surprised her. He looked so natural in them, just like his army fatigues. *I guess it didn't matter what he wore. He always seemed at ease, comfortable in his own skin.*

"You have to meet my parents sometime. Why not now?" Devan asked with a slow, sexy smile.

"Why not later?"

"Always the procrastinator."

Devan grabbed Terra's hand, threading his fingers through hers, then dragged her through the doorway into the restaurant before she could protest further. The smell of fresh-baked bread hit her as soon as they crossed the threshold. It took a few moments for her eyes to adjust to the dim lighting. Her high heels clicked on the ceramic flooring.

The hostess led them to a reserved room at the back of the steakhouse. Terra exhaled when she realized the room was empty. The hostess seated them, took their drink order, and left them alone.

Devan kept peeking at his watch. He sent a few texts but didn't get any responses. "It's not like them to be late. They are normally an hour early for everything."

"Traffic, maybe. Military transports are slowing everything down." Terra offered. "There are a lot of those in town these days."

A few minutes later, the hostess delivered an envelope and a basket of freshly baked rolls.

Devan opened the note, shook his head, crumpled it up and tossed it on the table.

"What's wrong?" Terra broke open a bun and lavishly buttered it.

"See for yourself, my parent's plane has a problem with the landing gear. They can't take off."

"Oh no, I'm so sorry. I know you were looking forward to seeing them. Can they book a later flight?" Terra would have been relieved if she hadn't seen the disappointment on Devan's face.

Terra scanned the note. They said they were sorry to miss his birthday; they had tried calling and texting but couldn't get through. Terra had noticed that cell service had been getting worse lately. She glanced at her phone and noticed there was no signal.

The server interrupted to take their food order. Devon ordered the Prime Rib with double mashed potatoes and extra gravy. While Terra ordered the filet mignon with a twice-baked potato. Tomorrow she would eat a salad.

"Yeah, no. They weren't flying commercial; they have their own plane."

"You're kidding, right? Their own plane. How rich are they?" Terra hadn't grown up poor as a child of two doctors, but they didn't own a private jet.

Devan considered the question "Ridiculously rich."

"I thought your dad was ex-military."

"Yeah, he was a navy pilot for 25 years before he retired, but he came from a wealthy family who believed in service. He inherited a pile of money when his parents died."

"Must be rough." The corner of her lips raised in a smile.

"It is, thanks," Devan raised his brow. "But it gets worse.. my mom has money too. Her dad owned a jewellery store chain. When she started working there, she took the business from 10 stores to a chain of over 2500 nationwide."

"Wow, that is worse. I feel so sorry for you." Terra's mouth fell open slightly. "Do you have plans to work there after the military?"

"No," He scoffed. "Plus, she is in the middle of selling the business to Kay Jewelers. They want to travel and see stuff. Plus, I'm never leaving the military."

"I've heard of Kay Jewelers." Terra's stomach rumbled. She debated if she should eat another roll before her meal came.

"Yeah, they still want my mom to design for them, but she's not sure if she wants to yet."

"I didn't know she was a designer. Tell me more."

"Um, she started working for my grandpa when she was young, just had a knack for it, really. She took some design classes and stuff. But what about your parents? They were doctors, right?"

"When they were alive, Dad was an oncologist, mom a psychiatrist. Tess, my sister, is a nurse studying to become a doctor."

"I guess neither of us is interested in the family business," Devan said. A half-grin played at his lips.

"Not even slightly."

A server came with their meals.

"Guess who I met this week?" Devan asked.

"Can I have a hint?" Terra asked.

He shook his head.

"Beyonce," Terra guessed as she buttered another roll. They were addicting and she couldn't resist them. "Some General I've never heard of."

"How about the President of the United States?" Devan said.

"You met the President, the actual President." Terra's eyes lit up; her hand flew up to touch her heart necklace. "I voted for him. His wife, Sofia, is my idol. Did you get to meet her? I heard her give a lecture once on first amendment rights. It was earth-shattering."

"Not only did I get to meet her. Drum roll, please." Devan drummed on the table. "I carried her luggage to their room. Apparently, they are staying for a month."

"That's strange, the President never stays in one place that long besides the White House or Camp David." Terra said. Her reporter instincts were screaming at her to pay attention. She was missing something.

"I don't know."

"What's going on up at the military base, anyway?" Terra asked. She constantly pestered Devan for details. "Trucks going through town at all hours of the day and night. Two nights ago, I had to go the entire way around Colorado Springs to get to my apartment. It's ridiculous."

"As I keep telling you, the military runs on a need-to-know basis and privates don't need to know much," He laughed.

"But aren't you curious? Why is the President at the Cheyenne Mountain Complex? Is NORAD getting some new equipment?" Terra asked.

"It's classified."

Terra mouthed the words at the same time. It was the answer to every question she asked about the base. Her journalistic itch told her there was something going on. It had never steered her wrong before.

"You've been inside, right? What is it like? Does it feel claustrophobic? All that stale air."

"The air isn't stale. They clean it through blast valves using a filter system designed to screen for chemical, biological or radioactive agents." Devan explained.

"That still sounds stale to me. Do they give tours?" Terra asked. Living outside the base for her entire life, she had always wanted to get inside.

"Not since September 11th, 2001," Devan answered. "That's the last time the blast doors were closed for more than daily testing."

Servers came out singing Happy Birthday, carrying a three-tiered chocolate cake with 24 burning candles. Devan's cheeks heated. "My parents are not even here and they are embarrassing me."

After dinner, Terra and Devan took a long slow stroll around the park, hand in hand. Terra held her shoes in her free hand. The grass tickled her bare feet. She shivered, so Devan took off his coat and wrapped it around her shoulders. The nights were getting warmer as they neared the summer.

Just as they approached an intersection, the sound of brakes squealing followed by a loud crash caught their attention. One of the big army trucks had driven through a red light into the intersection and t-boned a small blue Chevy Cruz, trapping it between the pet food store and the green M-939 truck.

Devan dropped Terra's hand and scrambled to help. Terra followed, shrugging off the coat and dumping her heels and purse. She cursed as the stones bit into the soles of her bare feet.

Devan reached the driver of the truck first. The windshield had shattered. Devon opened the door for the driver. His eyes were open. He sat there stunned as blood oozed from a cut above his right eye. Devan helped the driver out of the truck before he waved him towards the car.

Terra wondered why the truck and driver were alone. The trucks normally appeared in convoys with two people in the front cab.

The frame of the Cruz was twisted beyond repair. The hood had crumpled like an accordion when the car hit the structure. The driver hadn't moved.

As Devan neared the car, Terra spotted a trail of fuel leaking from the gas tank. Without noticing, the driver of the truck lit a cigarette and dropped the match on the ground, igniting the fuel. When he realized what he had done, he looked on in horror before he turned and ran.

Her mouth opened before she could warn Devan. The car exploded in a ball of flames, rising off the ground before falling back on its wheels. The explosion threw Devan back violently. He landed hard on the pavement, his shoulder receiving the brunt of the force.

The roar of the explosion caused a ringing in Terra's ears. She screamed Devan's name as she ran to him. The fire burned hot as the smoke poured out of the vehicle. It was too late for the driver of the car; nothing could have survived the explosion. Glass and metal dug into her feet, but nothing would deter her from getting to Devan.

Terra dropped beside Devan. Checking him for injuries. His eyes were open, but he wasn't moving, conscious but stunned. The heat from the fire baked her from the inside out. Terra checked the back of Devan's head, and her hand came away sticky with blood.

She needed to move him back from the fire. Her hands struggled to grab him underneath his shoulders. She pulled with all her might, but he was too heavy for her to drag. Her eyes searched for the truck driver, but he had disappeared in the smoke.

As a reflex, Terra checked her pockets for her phone until she remembered she was in a dress. "Don't move. I'll be right back." She cursed as she raced back to where she had dropped her purse and shoes, then dug out her phone and dialled 911.

Devan propped himself up on one elbow.

She ran back as she talked to the 911 operator, noticing the trail of blood she had left behind. Every step she took, the debris dug deeper into her feet. The heat from the fire was intense. She put up her hand to shield her face as she skirted around pieces of the exploded Cruz. "Lie back down," Terra yelled.

"We need to move. The M-939 could blow too," Devan's eyes opened and closed. He had trouble focusing.

With a Herculean effort, Terra helped him to his feet. He looped his arm around her, using her as a crutch. They crossed the road back into the park. With Terra's help, he lowered himself to the ground beside a bench, holding his head between his hands.

The driver of the truck reappeared. Agitated, he waved his hands in the air. Tears rolled down his cheeks, but he did not wipe them away. He bent over at the waist, retching. When he finished, he kept saying "It's all my fault" over and over.

Using her free hand, Terra folded up Devan's suit jacket. She coaxed him to lie down, placing his head on the makeshift pillow. Sirens wailed in the distance. It wouldn't take long for the fire department to arrive, they were only a few blocks over. Terra reconnected with a 911 operator who reassured her someone had already called in the explosion.

Terra sat beside Devan and turned her attention to her bloody feet. She pulled some of the bigger pieces out, causing fresh blood to pour out of her wounds. She ripped a piece off the bottom of her dress and applied pressure to the deepest cuts, all the while monitoring Devan.

Road rash covered Devan's right arm from his landing. He tried to speak.

"Just stay still until the paramedics get here. You probably have a concussion. I don't know how badly your head is bleeding."

The truck driver wandered closer, fresh blood drenched the top of his uniform. Terra ripped another strip from the bottom of her dress and handed it to the driver, telling him to put pressure on his wound.

"I didn't see... she came out... of nowhere... I didn't mean... I killed her... I killed that girl...," The driver rambled. "Had to get away... get my family... save my family... before it comes."

"I'm a fellow soldier... on the base." Devan winced as he spoke. "You need to call this in. Follow protocols."

"Calm down, it's okay. It was an accident." Terra spoke tenderly to the driver. Terra pushed the hair back from Devan's eyes. She knew he had a concussion, but she hoped that was all. Where was the ambulance? Why wasn't it here yet?

"Who are you talking to?" The driver came closer and slapped the phone out of Terra's hand. It flew five feet before it hit a parking meter and exploded into pieces.

"Hey, what the—?" Terra was beyond angry. She had enough to deal with without this crazy truck driver.

The streets had become congested because the army truck blocked the intersection. A crowd had formed behind them, watching the commotion. People had their cell phones out, taking photos, videos and talking. The firetruck finally arrived, and the firefighters scrambled into action. It was only a matter of minutes, but it felt like forever.

When a police car arrived, the driver looked around wildly. He stepped away before turning around and crouching down. In a low, rough voice, he said, "The end of the world is coming. A giant asteroid. You need to find shelter..." He bounced to his feet, pushed through the crowd, and disappeared.

CHAPTER FIVE

Terra
June 27, 2049 11:49 am

Terra and Tess lined up behind the barricades, outside the gates at the Cheyenne Mountain Complex, along with roughly ten thousand other people. Between the barricades and the fence line stood rows of soldiers in riot gear, rifles up, pointing at the growing crowd. Snipers occasionally fired off a round when the gathering got too close to the fence.

Drones flew over the assembly of people looking for those desperate enough to approach the fence line. After snipers shot the third runner dead, the attempts to run the fence declined. Those that still tried met the same fate.

A soldier with a megaphone kept repeating the same phrase. "Do not approach the fence line without a military escort. Authorized personnel are directed to the red tent with the white X. All others must leave this facility."

Protesters yelled, "Hell no, we won't go".

A jumbotron showed video footage from around the world. Meteoroid strikes had already taken out Paris, Philadelphia, Shanghai, Nepal, Vancouver and the entire island of Japan. Smaller meteorites had fallen with more regularity as Attila drew closer. Sometimes they created spectacular fireballs when they hit the earth's atmosphere, but other times they did deadly damage when they touched the surface, igniting fires that ran rampant. The world was burning. Seismic shocks rippled through the earth's surface, toppling buildings.

Terra and Tess had battled their way through the gathering, shoving their way to the front. Until terra worried the desperation of the crowd would crush them against the heavy cement barricade, so they backed away and went over to the red tent and waited in a line. They had already trampled people to death.

Soldiers at a makeshift desk created from the tailgate of a jeep screened people. Fitting those authorized with a wrist bracelet.

Terra checked her watch. Less than twelve hours until the scheduled time for Attila to arrive at 11:35 pm. A soldier called for Terra to approach the desk.

"Name," the soldier said without glancing up. A dozen soldiers stood behind him, guns drawn, heads on a swivel, looking for all potential threats.

"T... Terra Baxter. I'm looking for my boyfriend, Devon. Private Devon Edge, he works here." Terra's mouth was so dry she had trouble getting the words out, her voice came out scratchy from yelling over the crowd trying to communicate with Tess and the throng of military personnel.

"Lady, this line is for people approved for entry." The soldier scowled at her. He looked past her and yelled. "Next."

"I know that, but I'm trying to find him. I thought he might be inside." Terra bit the inside of her cheek hard until she tasted blood. "Could you check Sergeant Grimaldi... please?"

"Lady, nobody has time to look for him. If he is here, then he's working. Look around you. It's a nightmare." The soldier raised his chin towards the armed soldiers behind him. "Move or they'll move you."

"I'm not leaving here until somebody helps me find him." Terra placed her hand over her heart. She felt a tightening in her chest. Was she having a heart attack? "I need to find him; I have something important to tell him."

Tess pulled at Terra's arm "Come on, let's go before we get in trouble." Tess's eyes looked overly bright, feverish. She tugged again.

"Move along," the soldier barked.

"Please Terra," Tessa begged.

"What can they do with us? Attila is going to kill us today." Terra turned back towards the soldier. "Must be nice to know you have a place inside the bunker."

"Lady, I don't, most of us here, don't," He bit off every word, his face turning red "Countless soldiers have already deserted. Maybe your boyfriend is one of those. NOW, move along or somebody who hasn't deserted yet will shoot you."

"You don't know him. Devan would never do that. Thanks for nothing." Terra threw her hands up and gave his two middle fingers, then turned away from the red tent as Tess followed. She stopped to pull a pack of gum from the pocket of her jeans, offering a piece to her sister. Popping bubbles always seemed to calm her.

Terra hadn't heard from Devan since the truck driver had dropped the news about the asteroid. The paramedics hadn't allowed her in the ambulance since she had her own wounds to get treated. Then, by the time she arrived at the hospital and had the debris removed from her feet, soldiers had taken Devan straight to the base.

It had taken a lot of persuasion for Tess to come with her to the base. Tess had convinced herself the government would come up with a last-minute plan to save them, so she resisted at first. She was content to sit on the couch watching a twenty-four-hour news channel on Armageddon.

The news of 'Attila' the asteroid broke two weeks ago. Terra was pulling the threads of the story together when a political reporter working for CNN beat her to it. There was still a lot of speculation on just how long the Government had been aware of the asteroid.

The world had gone crazy. Some people flocked to religion, while others looted stores, finally getting the gigantic television screen they had always wanted. Other people lived in denial, keeping to their daily routine, still going to work in empty office buildings, with days left to live.

Terra and her sister had gone through the five stages of grief. Denial that the asteroid existed. Anger that there was nothing they could do to stop it. They bargained with God and every other deity that they could think of. Then came depression and finally acceptance. They had exhausted themselves crying and reached the part where they were numb. As a last resort, they had come to the base hoping for a miracle or to find Devan. Terra had something she desperately need to tell him.

Tess wiped the sweat from her forehead before replacing her Colorado Avalanche Stanley Cup Champions ball cap. The sun beamed down on them with all its glory. Terra knew from her research that after today she might never see the sun again. The asteroid dust would block it for years, freezing the planet.

Terra's t-shirt was damp, plastered against her back from the steady stream of perspiration. She felt agitated, like she was in the center of a storm. Her jaw was sore from chomping on gum.

Fresh soldiers came out of the arched door of the complex. Was it a shift change or reinforcements? The door seemed tiny compared to the mountain, but it was big enough to drive large military vehicles through, and then some. The noise level, which was already at its peak, rose a notch as the people outside the fence pleaded for their lives with the new arrivals. Children of all ages stood with their parents, a sense of hopelessness surrounding them. Some parents had tried to hand their children to the soldiers, begging for their lives.

Terra scanned the soldiers, searching for Devan. They all looked the same, dressed in military fatigues, with patrol hats pulled low.

"Do you see him?" Tess yelled in Terra's ear.

Terra shook her head. What would she do if she did? She alternated between worry about his injury to anger that he ghosted her. She had stupidly thought she loved him. Terra grunted as an elbow struck her ribs. This wasn't working. They were going to get swallowed up in this crowd. It was a riot in the making. The closer they got to Attila's arrival, the worse it would be.

Soldiers strode up and down the fence line, their faces as hard as the granite of the mountain. Oblivious to all the pleas of the people. This was a colossal waste of time. They would not open the gates and jeopardize those already inside, those chosen few.

Terra jumped up and down, looking for a safer spot. She noticed a barricade further down the fence line with fewer people crowded around it. Hanging onto Tess's arm like a vice, she pulled her along as they made their way through the crowd, shoving and pushing every step of the way. Tess fell to her knees after being thrust sideways. She screamed in panic, but Terra pulled her back on her feet.

The new area was less crowded than the main gate. There were two guards speaking to the public when they arrived. Neither of them had heard of Devan or knew how to contact him when Terra finally got to speak to them, but they were nicer than the guy at the red tent. From what she could hear, anyway.

"Maybe we should go home, spend the rest of our time together there," Tess shouted into her ear. "I don't want to be here anymore."

Terra scanned the soldiers, searching hopelessly for Devan. She picked up her phone and tried calling him for the umpteenth time. Cell service hadn't worked for days. "You're right, we should go. They will never let us in." She didn't want to give up, but finding him seemed pointless. She chomped hard on her gum.

Some instinct told her to look up. The guards were changing; two other soldiers, one man and a woman, replaced them. The way one of them walked seemed familiar. Terra inched closer for a better look.

"Where are you going?" Tess asked, following behind her sister. "I thought we were leaving."

Terra held up a finger. "Just one sec. I need to check something." She screamed. "Devan. Devan. DEVAN." She was too far away; he would never hear her. She locked her eyes on him, willing him to look in her direction.

Devan looked up. His eyes met Terra's from under his patrol hat, full of relief and love. He mouthed her name, but the crowd swallowed up his words. The five feet between them may have been a hundred with the number of people between them. He waved her towards him.

Terra yelled. "You're okay." Like a madwoman, she elbowed her way closer, dragging her sister behind her.

Devan looked fine to her, but concussions were tricky. He put his hand to his ear, letting her know he couldn't hear her over the pack. He tried to get closer to Terra, but people noticed Devan speaking with her and fought for his attention. One man held up wads of cash. What good was money now?

Tess said nothing as she followed along, but she studied Devan with suspicion and hope.

Devan waved her forward. As soon as she was close enough, he seized her in a bear hug. He pressed his mouth against her ear. She couldn't make out the words at first, but he kept repeating them until she finally understood. "Get... break... fence."

Devan released her, then put his hand beside his head as if he were making a call and mouthed the word 'family'. Terra nodded. He pointed to his watch and 9:00 pm before turning back to his partner. Looking back over his shoulder, Devan gave her a nervous smile before a hand gripped his shoulder spinning him around, pulling him away

Terra motioned to Tess that they needed to leave. She grabbed Tess's sweaty hand so they wouldn't get separated. It was much easier to get out than it was to get in.

Once they were far enough away to speak, Terra explained what Devan asked her to do before making a call.

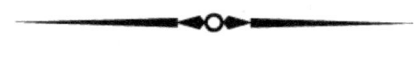

Sofia
6:32 pm

"Mom, are you sure? Maybe it's too risky. You shouldn't go tonight." Joe asked Sofia.

"Attila is going to arrive in a few hours. Stay here, where you are safe. Dad will go crazy if he can't find you." Rob scrubbed his hand across his face. He looked so much like James when he did that.

"The same if he can't find you. Don't think you're going without me. It's our last chance to breathe fresh air for a long time, and I'm not about to miss it. We have plenty of time to get out and back, with time to spare." Sofia checked her watch. It was just after 6:30 pm. "Besides, I would just worry about you the entire time knowing you were out there. I know we shouldn't do this, but—"

"You need to see it one more time." Joe completed her sentence. "I feel you."

Sofia, Joe and Rob had been sneaking out for the last month as often as they could get away. Security had caught them twice, and James was less than impressed. He needed them safe and sound inside the hollowed-out mountain. They tried using the dogs as an excuse until James reminded them that he had Astra-turf installed for that very reason. James even threatened them with restoring their secret service coverage if they didn't behave.

Sofia nodded. "Just one last time." She knew better, but she couldn't resist. Thousands of people wished they were in her shoes. Safe inside a military bunker but it was a small high every time they broke protocol, giving Sofia the rush, she needed right now. A way to feel alive.

They were quiet as they made their way through the facility and out of the residences to the main tunnel exiting from the personnel entrance. They had to show their security badges at several points, but no one tried to stop them. The entire world knew they were the first family.

The thin black metal badges were worth their weight in gold; the most valuable things in the world right now. There was less security inside since they needed more security at the perimeter. Everybody inside already had clearance; had been picked for a purpose.

Even from this distance, Sofia could hear the sounds of the people outside the facility. She had heard there were tens of thousands of people, but she couldn't go near the fence or she would let everyone in. She would break down. It was cowardice to avoid them, but she knew she would melt into a puddle of tears.

Not that making it inside would guarantee their safety, but at least it was a chance. She didn't like the thought of playing God. Who were they to decide who lives and who dies?

The bunker had become packed as the government installed their list of VIPs. The list included top government officials, doctors, paramedics, engineers, specialists of every kind. People that would be useful in helping society to rebuild after. People that could be creative, working with the materials they had on hand in case of the worst scenario and it trapped there them for years. The bunker would accommodate 800 people easily during wartime, but only 500 were moving in.

In the main tunnel, parked military vehicles sat in rows in the vehicle turnaround. Rob jumped inside a growler with an open top and started it up before Joe and Sofia got in. For once they didn't argue about who would drive. Exiting the tunnel, Rob pointed the growler away from the main gate and drove it up into the hills. The wind felt good as the cool air fanned her face. Sofia stared sightlessly at the passing scenery.

Rob parked the growler partway up the mountain and they got out to stretch their legs. Sofia sucked in a deep breath. The air inside the complex left a bitter taste and an antiseptic smell. At times she felt that life inside the complex was like being buried alive.

The Hollows had become a nickname for their new home. It started as a joke, but a lot of things start that way. She wondered how long the confinement in the hollowed-out mountain would last. Scientists had estimated months to years. This was an unprecedented event, so no one really knew anything.

An electrical storm sent ribbons of light through the sky. Lighting with no thunder or rain.

CHAPTER SIX

Terra

June 27, 2049 6:44 pm

Terra contacted Devan's family just as he had asked. Using their private jet, they arrived just after dark flying 497 miles from El Paso, Texas. The government had grounded all planes, but Matthew, Devan's father, risked taking off, hoping that the air force wouldn't shoot him down. He avoided flying over the base and landed at the abandoned Colorado Springs airport.

If Terra wanted to know what Devan would look like when he got older, she only needed to look at Matthew. Though his hair was grayer than brown now. They had the same facial features. Sandra had red hair with a freckled complexion. She had a look on her face that said, 'I will punch you if you cross me.' This wasn't the circumstances I had envisioned for my introduction to Devan's parents.

"What if we get to the location and he's not there? Then what?" Tess asked. "What if they fixed the fence, you said he reported it?"

"We are bringing bolt cutters just in case." Terra busied herself repacking her backpack, trying to squeeze in everything she could. She talked tough, but she was a bundle of nerves.

"What if we can't cut through the fence?" Tess drew her bottom lips through her teeth.

"Then we get creative."

"How do we get creative?"

"Damn it, I don't know, Tess, I don't have all the answers," Terra poked a tongue into her cheek and exhaled. "All I know is that I would rather die doing something instead of dying doing nothing."

Tess's shoulders dragged low, and her arm lost all tension. She looked away, her eyes blinking back rising tears.

Terra cursed under her breath, but before she could apologize Matthew tapped her shoulder, causing her to jump. "What?"

"I think we are ready," Matthew adjusted the straps on his backpack before he hoisted his wife's bag. Sandra carried a powerful flashlight that would help them find their way after the sunset faded to darkness. They both wore necklaces, rings, and watches. Jewelry adorned fingers, arms, and necklines. Were they hoping that jewelry would equal currency?

The hike would be hard for them, but they could relax once they were inside and safe. Terra mentally prepared herself to do whatever it took to get them all to the meeting point.

"Do you think you can find this place again?" Sandra asked.

Sandra's hiking boots and loose clothing made her almost unrecognizable from the photos Terra had seen. Devan said she normally wore business attire. He had never seen his mother in anything else, or so he said. She always came down for breakfast fully dressed and stayed that way until she went to bed.

Terra wondered how Sandra and Matthew would react to her secret. She wished she had time to tell Devan earlier. She had been building up to it before the accident. Although then she wasn't sure then, but now she was.

The electrical storm that had started earlier was getting worse. Peculiar ribbons of lights crossed the sky. Lighting with no thunder or rain.

Sofia
6:48 pm

From their vantage point on Cheyenne Mountain, Sofia could see the city of Colorado Springs sprawled out below.

"What do you think they are doing there?" Joe had a pair of binoculars in his hands as he peered down at the city.

"I can't imagine what they are going through. How scared they are. It breaks my heart..." Sofia turned her face away from the boys so they couldn't see her expression. A wave of nausea hit her, but she fought it.

"Freaking out." Rob lowered the tailgate of the growler so they could sit. He offered a hand to Sofia. "What else would you expect?"

They had called the National Guard to deal with the first of the riots, but with limited time remaining, they had deserted their posts, and the United States had fallen into lawlessness. Soldiers inside the base had stayed, but many others had deserted to spend their last days with their loved ones.

"What will all this look like tomorrow?" Joe picked up a limb and drew stick people in the dirt. "Will there still be mountains? Will we be underwater?"

"Don't let your mind get ahead of you. One day, one moment at a time." Sofia said.

"Mindfulness, really mom?" Rob raised an eyebrow.

"Don't knock it till you try it." Sofia had been practicing it a lot lately, along with deep breathing and reciting the serenity prayer. She had made sure that James installed people inside to help with mental health. They would all need it.

Terra
6:50 pm

All eyes flew to the sky as the whoosh of rotating helicopter blades caught their attention. The chopper flew along the fence line in the other direction, looking for intruders. The base embedded in Cheyenne Mountain had too much fenceline to cover on foot, so drones and Helicopters surveyed the perimeter.

"That was close. We need to steer away from the fence as much as possible to keep out of range. Then veer in once darkness falls in about an hour. Can you do that, Terra?"

"I'll get us there." Terra's muscles tightened as she threw her pack over her shoulder. Somehow, she would get them where they needed to go. There was no alternative. She turned and led the way, with Matthew by her side.

Sofia
7:15 pm

"Mom, are you okay?" Rob asked softly. He grew still to observe his mother better. "You haven't been yourself since dad became President."

"You don't have to be strong for us. It's okay to be depressed." Joe's eyes mirrored his brother's concern.

"I have no reason to be depressed." Sofia angled her body away from her boys, blinking back the tears that welled in her eyes from their kindness. "No more reason than anyone else, I mean."

"Mom, you feel what you feel," Rob said. "You don't have to be embarrassed about it. Everybody feels it sometimes."

"I know, but with all my privileges, depression can't be something I have, not with countless others—." Sofia pressed her hands against her cheeks.

"Depression hits everyone regardless of wealth or privilege," Joe said. "Think of all the celebrities who have money, fame and anything else they could want. They suffer from depression too."

"Mom, this is a lot for anyone to deal with, even Sofia freaking Cutter," Rob said.

"I feel like I haven't been Sofia freaking Cutter in a long time. Since I was on the Harvard Law review, made partner before 30 or advocated for anything other than a political campaign." She had felt so lost for so long.

"Mom—" Rob started before the sound of helicopter blades chopping captured his attention.

Terra
8:45 pm

"Are you sure this is the place?" Matthew asked.

"Positive," Terra answered, snapping her gum.

It took them longer to find the spot than Terra thought. All the trees looked alike, plus the looming darkness didn't help. They only had flashlights to help them navigate. Plus, the ragtag group of hikers questioned her every move. Especially Matthew, the retired navy pilot. If she had to hear one more story about his Navy flying days, she was going to scream.

"Drone, everybody down." Matthew barked the order a split second before a flash of light and a high-pitched buzzing overhead drew their attention.

They all scrambled to hide in the brush or under a tree until the drone passed by. Terra didn't know how Matthew had even heard it. The wind had picked up, blowing hotter as the day went on.

"Do you think it saw us?" Terra asked.

"No, I don't think so. It would have fired; military drones have that capability." Matthew checked his watch "Where's Devan? Where is my son?"

"He'll be here." Terra fidgeted with the straps of her backpack. He still had 15 minutes to arrive before he would be late. She tried to call him, but her phone might have been a paperweight for all its use. She didn't know why she was still carrying it around with her.

"Are you sure this is the right place? All the trees and rocks look the same." Sandra looked exhausted from the hike. Dirt smudged her face, and she even had a twig stuck in her hair. She was a long way from Texas high society.

"I'm sure. This is the tree, and the fence is still waiting for repair." Terra pointed out the obvious.

Terra grabbed the cutters from where Matthew had dropped them and notched the cutters into a fence link to split the fence further. They had all taken turns dragging the heavy bolt cutters up the mountain, but not without complaints.

"Are we really doing this right now?" Tessa asked.

"We are. Even if Devan doesn't get here on time maybe we can find some back way into the complex."

"I know, but... I mean, this is military property, right? It feels wrong." Tess licked her lips before worrying her bottom lips between her teeth.

"I'm pretty sure it is illegal." Sandra kept a tight grip on the flashlight, pointing it wherever her imagination heard a noise. She shuffled her feet nervously.

"I'm pretty sure that the military has other problems to deal with right now. Like the world ending." Terra said. "The soldiers can't be everywhere."

"Who knows how many soldiers have already deserted? Isn't that what that guy by the red tent told you." Tess said.

Matthew nodded his head "This is the least of their worries. Go ahead."

Terra set to work opening the slice in the fence until her arms trembled and she handed the cutters off to Matthew. It was much tougher to cut than Terra thought it would be.

Sandra kept checking the sky as if the asteroid would appear momentarily, swinging the flashlight wildly

Sofia
9:00 pm

"Do you see that?" Joe pointed towards the fence.

"What," Sofia squinted but saw nothing.

"A flash of light. It looks like somebody is over there on the other side of the fence." Joe handed the binoculars to Sofia.

"Let me see," Rob said as he extended his hand.

Looking through the binoculars, Sofia saw a bunch of civilians. She handed the binoculars to Rob. "We better check it out on our way back. It's time to go, anyway." She took one last deep breath before climbing back into the growler.

Colorado Springs glowed as the last light of day gave way to the shadows of the sunset. An orange fireball streaked across the ebony sky and exploded on the other side of town, causing the ground to shake. There was an explosion and a fire ignited.

Terra
9:01 pm

Terra felt her heart clench in her chest as a fireball hit the ground near Colorado Springs. She quit breathing and stared. A piece of Attila had just eradicated part of the city, leaving it burning in flames. If that was just a piece, what would the entire asteroid do?

Terra shared a look with her sister. Had they just seen a preview of their fate?

Sandra's lips and chin trembled. Her freckles threatened to pop off her face. She reached for Matthew's hand, who stood with his mouth hanging open.

"It's okay dear, Devan is coming for us," Matthew absently took his wife's hand, patting it reassuringly, even if his face didn't believe a word he said.

Sofia
9:05 pm

As soon as the fireball hit Colorado Springs, Sofia knew they had made a mistake. What was she thinking? Stupid. Reckless. Risking safety for one last breath of fresh air.

Rob turned the motor over. The engine coughed, but the jeep wouldn't start. Sofia mentally panicked. James was going to kill her, and she deserved it. Her sons were at risk, and she had no one to blame but herself.

Rob tried again. Sofia heard the jeep click and grind.

"Stop it," Joe yelled. "You are going to flood the engine."

"No, I'm not." Rob yelled back as he turned the key one more time.

As if to prove Joe wrong, the engine turned over.

Sofia thanked the Universe, promising to do anything if she could just get her boys back to safety.

Terra

9:12 pm

Terra flinched at every sound in the dusk. She kept glancing at her watch every few seconds, as if that would make Devon get there faster. They didn't want to leave the area and miss him, but they might have to leave soon.

Sandra and Matthew chatted softly with Tess, but she couldn't focus on the conversation as she peered into stared into the distance.

She heard the noise long before she saw a set of lights from the vehicle approaching from inside the fence line.

"He's here." Terra reached for Tess's hand and squeezed.

"There he is." Matthew smiled with relief. "There's my boy. I told you, Sandra, that he would get here, didn't I?"

The jeep stopped, and three people exited. Two men and a woman, but not Devan.

Sofia

9:13 pm

"What do you think you are doing?" Sofia asked the group on the other side of the fence. She crossed her arms across her chest. Four people. A family maybe? One couple older than Sofia and two girls in their early twenties.

A girl with long dark hair in a ponytail stepped forward. "Mrs. Cutter, I can explain... it's not what it looks like" she wrung her hands together, nervously.

"Really, because it looks like you are destroying government property." Rob stood with his hands on his hips. A grin playing at his lips

Joe said nothing, but his jaw clenched as he kept checking his watch.

"I'm an ex-navy pilot..." an older gentleman with a Texas accent spoke.

The whup-whup-whup whirling chopping sound of another military vehicle approaching took everyone's attention. A helicopter. Everyone hit the ground a split second before guns fired. Spotlights from the helicopter tried to locate the group on the ground.

Sofia didn't recognize the sound of the first metal ping but she screamed in pain as a bullet pierced her arm. She dropped, then rolled and rolled until she hit a bush. The prickly points dug into her skin. Her heart raced so fast it caused pains in her chest. She curled up in a ball, making herself as small as possible. She couldn't see her boys. She couldn't see anything but dust. She has afraid to yell out to the boys in case she made them a target

Terra

9:15 pm

Terra hit the ground when the bullets started flying, getting a mouth full of dirt. The electrical storm flashed silver in the inky night sky, picking up intensity. She blinked at the dust the helicopter kicked up from her eyes and spit, the odd granule remained. Where was her sister? She had heard a woman scream. Was that Tess?

Straining her eyes, she could make out Matthew's body lying a couple of feet away. He wasn't moving. Terra rolled onto her belly, then pulled herself up on all fours and crawled closer.

The helicopter left after firing several rounds of bullets. Whether it was out of ammunition, they thought they removed their target or they needed the chopper someplace else... Terra didn't know.

Before Terra felt Matthew's neck for a pulse, she knew he was dead. A bullet had pierced his forehead. A noise from the left drew her attention, but it was only Tess hiding behind a boulder with Sandra. Sandra's hand covered her mouth as she cried. Sobs trembled from the sobs that wracked her body as she stared at her husband in horror.

Sofia

9:17 pm

Sofia felt a burning in her left forearm. She reached over with her right hand and felt a sticky liquid. Senses sharpened with adrenaline, she strained to hear her boys call out. Swirling dirt from the helicopter still hung in the air.

"Mom, mom?" Joe yelled.

"Mom, where are you? Mooooom..." Rob called.

"O... over here," Sofia called out. She could make out the outline of the boys under the jeep.

"Mom, are you okay?" Joe yelled.

"Y... yes, but I think they... shot me." Sofia struggled to sit up. She felt dizzy.

Joe raced to Sofia. He turned on the flashlight from his phone to inspect the damage. Tenderly probing the area around the wound and flipping her arm around to see the back. "You're lucky? The bullet went right through." Joe Adjuster her body until she was laying prone and then put his knee hard against the wound.

Sofia grunted from the pain. "Lucky?"

"What are you doing?" Rob looked towards the fence where the others had stood once he had assured himself his mother was okay.

"Putting pressure on the wound."

"Like that?"

"Yeah, I know what I'm doing."

"Okay then, you got this." He glanced away then looked back. "I'll check on the others."

"Yeah, sounds good... just get me the first aid kit from the jeep before you go."

"Growler."

"Whatever."

Sofia heard Rob as he thumped through the jeep. He ran back and tossed Joe a first aid kit. Sofia watched as he disappeared. She glanced up at the sky, listening for the chopper to return to finish the job. Sofia felt something that she hadn't felt in a long-time, white-hot rage.

Terra
9:20 pm

Tess sat with Sandra as she cried for her husband, trying to comfort her. Being a nurse, Tess was much better at that kind of thing than Terra.

Terra checked her watch. She couldn't believe only thirty-five minutes had passed since they arrived here. Turning on the high-powered flashlight, she searched to see what had happened to the first lady and her boys.

She heard a voice call out. "Is everybody okay over there?"

"No, we... we have a casualty... my boyfriend's dad is... dead!" Terra hurried over to find one twin with his fingers entwined in the fence. "What about your side of the fence, everyone safe?"

"They shot my mom, but she is going to be okay. Joe is looking after her." He gave a short laugh "I feel sorry for whoever shot her when my dad finds out. What is your name?"

"Terra, Terra Baxter." At least now she knew she was speaking with Rob. She felt tongue-tied. As if her fingers had a mind of their own, they played with the zipper of her sweatshirt.

Rob spotted the bolt cutters laying on the ground. "Could you hand me those?"

Terra watched as he made quick work cutting a bigger hole in the fence. He rolled back a section large enough for them to walk through.

"Is the rest of your party ambulatory?" Rob asked. "Because we need to get out of here in case that chopper returns."

"Yes, I think so." Terra exhaled and closed her eyes. He wouldn't leave them here to fend for themselves. "Why do you think, the chopper left?"

"No clue." Rob strolled over to Sandra and helped her to her feet while Terra and Tess gathered the backpacks.

"Can you get his jewellery? We might need it." Sandra swiped at her eyes to remove the moisture.

"Really?"

Sandra nodded.

It made Terra's skin crawl to touch Matthew's dead body, but she did as Sandra asked.

Sofia
9:25 pm

Sofia felt much better after Joe stopped the bleeding and wrapped her arm in gauze. The wound stung and throbbed, and the Advil from the first aid kit didn't help.

"Joe, I think the tires on the growler are flat." Sofia had been staring at it while he patched her up.

"I noticed." Joe wiped the blood from his hands on his pant legs. "We are about five miles away, so we need to get moving. Can you walk?"

"Yes, I was shot in the arm, not the foot, help me to my feet." Sofia raised her good hand.

Joe avoided her hand but instead placed his body under her shoulder to give her leverage in case she fell.

"Do you think we will make it back in time?"

Joe worried his bottom lip between his teeth and shrugged.

Sofia looked at the cracked screen of her phone. "Can you call your dad?" Sofia asked.

"No, the phones aren't working anymore, they haven't for days. You know that."

"What about the radio in the growler?"

"Nope, a bullet from the helicopter took it out too."

"I'm so sorry. I shouldn't have allowed this. What was I thinking?" Sofia wiped her hand across her face. "What kind of mother puts her children in jeopardy."

"It wasn't just you. We all decided."

Sofia's head snapped up when she heard a branch break, but it was just Rob returning with the three women. The older woman's eyes were red and swollen with tears. What had happened to her husband?

The wind picked up, blowing stronger, moving anything that wasn't pinned down. A strip of lightning hit the ground, sending a rock into the windshield of the growler.

CHAPTER SEVEN

Terra
June 27, 2049 10:15 pm

T erra and the ragtag crew had made it over two miles walking when they heard the roar of a land vehicle approaching. Fear clutched Terra's heart. Would the soldiers shoot first or let them explain? Terra looked around for somewhere to hide, but there was nothing to shield them from whatever was coming, just rocks and scrub bushes.

When the vehicle stopped, Terra couldn't hide her relief when Devan stepped out of a Humvee. She was never so glad to see him before. Running towards him, she quickly covered the distance between them as he sprinted towards her. He closed his arms around her, and she held on tight. She never wanted to let him go.

All the emotions of the past few days bubbled up to the surface. Terra felt the tears run down her cheeks, but she wouldn't release Devan to wipe them away. She still hadn't told him her secret.

"I m sorry, I'm sorry, I'm so sorry, I thought I wouldn't get to you on time. I can't believe I found you. Are you okay?" Devan kissed her on the top of her head a dozen times, pulling her towards him as tightly as possible.

"Soldier," Rob called out.

"Soldier are we glad to see you," Sofia called out.

"We need a lift," Joe added.

Devan couldn't hide his shock when he finally pulled away from Terra and noticed the First Lady with her boys. His focus had been on Terra. His eyes took in the bloody bandage on her arm "Ma'am, are you injured?"

Reverting to soldier mode, he scanned everyone until he found his mother. Soundless tears dripped down her face. He glanced around. "Terra, where's my dad?"

Terra met his eyes briefly. "I'm sorry, he ah—."

"N... no." Devan stood statue still.

"I'm so... so sorry."

Devan froze for a moment before taking a step backward. His eyes blinked rapidly. When he opened his mouth to speak, his lips trembled, but no sound emerged.

Sofia
10:15 pm

"Soldier," Sofia yelled again. The poor boy shook from shock, but he would have to grieve later. "Wake up."

"At least now we have a ride." Rob had been too quiet on the walk; too still for a boy that normally burst with energy.

"Mom, we seriously have to go. Time is ticking away." Joe pointed at his watch. His dark eyes radiated with a fierce, uncompromising need to be heard.

"Soldier." Sofia hadn't overhead the young man's name.

"Sorry, ma'am. Private Devan Edge." The soldier snapped out of his funk. He saluted her with a trembling hand.

"Are you the man responsible for these people being out here on the mountain?" Sofia asked.

"Yes, ma'am." Devan swallowed hard. "I... have no excuses. When I saw her earlier, I knew... I had to try. I... couldn't leave them behind."

Sofia focused on the space between them, thinking. "Well, Private, what were you planning to do, sneak them into the bunker?"

Devan nodded. "Yes, ma'am."

"How did you plan on doing that, Private Edge, with all the security on base," Rob seemed more curious than anything.

"I, ah... hadn't got that far on my plan. There are so many new people, so much confusion," Private Edge said. "I thought maybe the entrance by the vehicle turn around or down by the south portal. I don't know, I thought if I could just get them inside somehow, I would worry about—."

"The consequences after." Joe finished Devan's sentence. He kept glancing at his watch nervously. "Mom, we really need to move."

"You can't leave us here to die." The older woman said. Her bottom lip quivered. One shoulder dropped in resignation. She clutched at the strand of pearls hanging around her neck. "Please don't leave us here."

Her son moved to comfort her.

Sofia raised an eyebrow. "What are you talking about? Of course, we won't leave you here. I'll get you into the complex. All three of you. Once they close the blast doors... then we will see if any of us survive Attila."

"Mom, no, you can't." Joe shook his head. "Dad will flip."

"Are you proposing we leave them? I'm not doing that, Joe. I won't." Sofia shook her head.

"Yes. No. I don't know." Joe rubbed the back of his neck.

"Joe, I'm with Mom on this. You know, the bunker has some empty rooms. 800 people is the approved minimum during a crisis and they have approved only 500 people for entry."

"But there are only so many supplies to go around," Joe added.

"Joe, it's the right thing to do. You know that...don't you?" Sofia reached out to squeeze his shoulder. "We have the best minds in the world inside the bunker, we'll figure out how to make the supplies last somehow."

Joe sucked in his lip and nodded.

"OK then, everyone in the Humvee. I'm sitting up front." Sofia said.

Terra
10:20 pm

Terra fidgeted with the sleeves of her sweatshirt. She had hoped that the First Lady wouldn't abandon them on the mountain, but until that moment, she didn't know her actual intentions towards them.

For all she knew, they could have been marching towards a jail cell or getting escorted outside the gates as soon as they got to the complex. At least now they had a chance.

She shared a look with her sister, then Devan, who was comforting his mother.

Sofia said. "You're driving soldier?" Rob helped her in so she wouldn't bump her arm and closed the door.

Terra walked over and picked up Sandra's bag. One less thing for her to worry about.

Sofia

10:35 pm

The Humvee ride back was quick. Sofia's knees shook with relief when they were safely back in the main tunnel of the facility again. She promised herself she would never do something that risky again. Crossing herself, she said a quick prayer.

Security stopped them at a new checkpoint that hadn't been there on the way out. Sofia, Rob, Joe, and Devan scanned their security badges.

"Ma'am, I can't let these three into the facility without the special black metal security badges. How did they even get this far?" The soldier had thick arms and no neck, a solid mass of muscle covered with brown skin.

"That doesn't matter. You need to allow their entry now." Sofia used her lawyer's voice. The one that commanded attention. She hadn't used it in so long, she had almost forgotten how.

"No ma'am. I cannot do that."

"I am the First Lady of the United States. On my authority, you need to let these people inside. Do I need to bother my husband, the President?"

Terra

10:45 pm

The First Lady of the United States used her authority to get them past security. Sofia had hidden the three of them in the water plant at first, then came back with thin black ID tags and taken them into the residences. She had sent Devan back to work with an order to keep quiet.

Sofia took them to an empty room Terra, Tess, and Sandra could share. It was small, with twin bunk beds that took up most of the space, but that didn't matter. They only had the clothes on their back and the supplies they carried in.

After living in Colorado Springs her entire life, Terra had pictured the inside of the facility a hundred times. The residences could have been an apartment anywhere in the world instead of 2000 feet below the earth's surface. A soldier had told her the building sat on giant springs that weighed a thousand pounds each when he escorted them to their quarters.

Devan knocked on their open door. He held a bottle of pills in his hand that the doctor had prescribed for Sandra. A light sedative. After making sure they settled his mother, he asked Terra to go for a walk. Devan reached for her hand and intertwined their fingers. His skin was warm and calloused.

"So, how are you doing? The truth. Not what you want me to hear." Terra watched his face for any micro-movements that would give away his genuine feelings.

His lips pressed together in a thin line. "I honestly don't know yet. Can't believe he's gone. We were never that close. Not really. He was always there, but not present. You know. In the Navy, he was always on deployment, on some ship in the middle of the ocean. The Navy was his entire focus. He loved me, I'm not saying he didn't, but he always had his own thing going on."

Terra raised her hand, placing it on his cheek. "I get it. My parents were doctors. They placed medicine before me and my sister more times than I care to remember. I get it was the right thing to do as doctors, but as parents, it sucked."

"It still feels surreal. This whole thing does. You can't believe how crazy things have been the last few weeks. I couldn't get out to see you or call you... or my parents. I thought the world would end without... without me seeing you again. I almost couldn't bear it." He brought the back of her hand to his lips and gave it a kiss.

"I know how you feel, we were so used to technology... to that instant connection... that I felt lost without it."

"And now you are here." He frowned. "Did you know that out of the five guys I work with, I was the only one selected? The only one given a security badge." He rubbed the back of his neck with his free hand.

"Selected for what?"

"For a spot inside the bunker. My friends, my brothers, didn't get selected. It was just random. My serial number came up. We all do the same job, but I get to live, and they don't."

"Kind of like winning the lottery."

"Yeah, no. It's nothing like that. It should feel that way, but it doesn't. It feels horrible, my stomach has been upset for days."

A television monitor on the wall broadcast the news. It was getting worse outside. Only in America would reporters work during the apocalypse. Terra's dream of breaking a big story as a reporter seemed silly now with everything else going on in the world.

"How long do you have? Maybe we shouldn't go too far? It's confusing in here and I don't want to get lost." Terra said.

"Pay attention to the trim colors on the buildings. You live in orange building seven. You'll get used to it. It takes a minute."

"I'm not worried. I'll figure it out." Terra rubbed a hand over her head and found a leaf. She must be a mess.

"I have to go back soon. The first lady said I could have an hour or two, but there is no off-duty right now. After the asteroid hits, if we survive... we have a briefing. Things are going to change. I shouldn't really be here I just wanted to talk to you first, in case...."

"That sounded ominous." Terra nibbled on her bottom lip, searching his eyes for any hint of what was coming. "It's okay, say it. I can take it."

"Take what," He narrowed his eyes, confused. "I know, it's quick and we haven't known each other very long, but... I love you, Terra. After what happened with my father, well, I don't know how much time we have left on this earth, but I want to spend what time we have left together. If we survive, I want to marry you."

Terra's eyes filled up with tears. She threw her arms around him in response. She whispered in his ear. "Devan, I'm pregnant. I know the timing couldn't be worse but..."

Devan pulled back his head so he could look her in the eye. "That's amazing. I don't know what is going to happen but we will face it together, the three of us." Devan's hands slipped down and stopped on her hips as he brought her body in closer. Neither of them noticed the crowd they drew as he lowered his head and kissed her.

Sofia
11:05 pm

"Mom, you need to have a real doctor look at your arm," Joe said. He grabbed for her good arm, but Sofia pulled away.

Sofia looked at her wrapped arm. It didn't appear any fresh blood had leaked through. "I will in a bit, but first I need you both to get to the control center. Your dad said it's the safest place in here."

"You need to be there too, mom." Rob said.

"I will I just have to do something first. Just go I'll be there before you know it."

"You better mom," A muscle in Rob's jaw twitched.

"Just go. The longer we stand here arguing, the longer it will take. Trust me. I'll be there. I promise."

"Ten minutes, mom, or we will come looking for you." Joe hooked his hair behind his ears.

"Yes, yes, I promise. Just go."

After they left, she took the Humvee down to the main gate so she could see what was happening for herself.

She mentally scolded herself for sticking her head in the sand these past weeks. It wasn't enough to save three people on the mountain when they could stretch their resources a little more.

When she reached the gate, the people begging for entry numbered in the thousands. One woman begged the soldiers to take her little girl holding the screaming child towards the soldier. All these people at the gate would die without help. With time running out the crowd had become more brazen pushing and shoving on the fence. With no other choice, the soldiers had begun firing on the people. She saw tears streaming from the eyes of more than one soldier as they did their duty.

Sofia didn't know what to do. If she opened the gate, they couldn't control the flood. There would be a stampede. But how could she choose who to save? And how?

She noticed a soldier walking past with tears running down his face and called him and four others to her side. "I need you to go through the crowd. Find families. All ages, all races. Load them into trucks and bring them in through the south portal where it's not as crowded. Do whatever it takes, do it discretely and quickly there isn't much time left but we are going to save some lives."

Sofia recruited other soldiers to help her. She had never abused her privilege as First Lady before, but she was making up for lost time now. She sent one to look for Terra, the girl she had rescued earlier. Terra had impressed her earlier with her ability to adapt to circumstances without falling apart. On their hike, Sofia walked with her, and they talked. She reminded Sofia of the person she used to be.

Terra
11:10 pm

A sergeant approached Devan as he escorted Terra back to the orange zone.

"Private, captain Campbell is searching for you. He needs your technical help in the command center ASAP."

"Right away, sir."

The soldier scurried on to another task.

Terra waved him away. "Go, go. I'll be fine. I'll find my way back."

"Are you sure?" He walked backwards away from her while talking

"Positive, we will both be here when you come back."

"Both of you. I like the sound of that."

Terra tried following the trim colors to her room. She eventually found her building, but before she could get back to her sister, a female soldier in a flight suit ordered Terra to accompany her.

Sofia
11:20 pm

Sofia enjoyed driving the growler, although the drive to the south entrance only took a few minutes. Sofia had to maneuver around mountains of supplies, although it was empty of people. Everyone inside was already at their appointed posts.

The soldier arrived with Terra in tow. "Madam, you sent for me?"

"Yes, I have sent soldiers on a brief rescue mission and I'm going to need help to move everyone, to find them housing and I do not know what else."

"Yeah, sure absolutely, anything I can do to help." Terra smiled widely.

"There you are, madam. The President is losing his mind looking for you. I need you to accompany me to the control center." Captain Campbell widened his stance, then placed his hands on his hips.

"How did you find me?" Sofia felt a fluttering in her stomach. Her chest tightened.

"The black security tags track your movements." The captain pushed his hat back and wiped the sweat from his brow.

Sofia could hear the M1078 trucks rumbling a few seconds before she saw the headlights of the first truck as it approached. "I will, but I need a little more time."

"Sorry madam but I am afraid that is an order, not a request."

"Well, Captain, short of throwing me over your shoulder, and carrying me away, you are just going to need to wait a bit. And don't even think about touching me." Sofia waved a finger in warning.

As the trucks arrived, soldiers helped everyone down out of the truck and directed them towards Sofia and the tunnels, urging them to hurry.

Sofia lost sight of the captain in the crowd. An older woman who spoke Spanish pushed a rosary into Sofia's hand. She inundated Sofia with hugs and words of thanks before the soldiers pulled her away.

Terra
11:25 pm

Terra stood too still and watched before she snapped out of it and helped Sofia get the newcomers out of the tunnel and into the bunker. One of the television screens showed soldiers shutting the blast doors. Terra felt nausea. Too many emotions swirled inside her. The survivor's guilt threatened to knock her to her knees as she saw the faces of these people left outside the complex. That could have been her.

Devan had told her the doors were so finely tuned it only took forty-five seconds for the hydraulics to swing the giant pistons into parallel slots. Engineers designed the doors to tighten like a plug sealing the bunker airtight. Terra wondered if it would be enough. No one could leave or enter the bunker for years.

Sofia
11:25 pm

James found Sofia a few minutes later, with Zhang and DeShawn tailing him. He pulled her to the side and hissed, "Sofia, what have you done? At what point did you think this was a good idea? We don't have the resources to accommodate all these people. I can't concentrate on my job while you're running around out here doing who knows what. You are worse than our kids. At least they have the sense to be in the control center where it is safe. And Joe tells me you've been shot. How is your arm?"

Sofia smiled up at James. "I'm sorry, I really am, but I couldn't stand by and do nothing anymore. You understand, right? You understand why I did what I did, don't you?"

"You're killing me." James clutched at his heart as if he were having a heart attack. As people streamed by, thanking them both. He shook his head, then took a deep breath. "What am I going to do with you and your soft heart?"

"So, you're not mad?" Sofia asked.

James scrubbed his hand across his face and closed his eyes. "I don't know how I feel, to be honest. We can sort that out later, but I need you to come with me right now and let the soldiers finish up here. I need you and the boys with me in the command center when Attila hits. Live or die, we need to be together. Afterward, you need to let a doctor look at your arm."

"Okay... James, you win."

"That was too easy. What else have you done?" James asked. He looked around as if Sofia had hidden an elephant in the tunnels. He knew she would have if she could.

Sofia felt better than she had since learning about the asteroid. She had done something she could feel good about. It wasn't enough, but it was something.

James put his arm around Sofia's shoulder and kissed her on the top of the head.

"James, can I ask you a question?"

"Sure, what?"

"Who killed JFK?"

James threw his head back and laughed.

"Are there really aliens at Area 51? What about Roswell? The world is ending. You don't have to keep things secret anymore, do you?"

Terra
11:30 pm

Terra was pulled along with Sofia into the command center. It was smaller than she expected, maybe 40 square feet. Eight gigantic TV screens blanketed the walls, showing the world and the asteroid approaching. The room was full of busy people moving around.

The softly dimmed light muted the blue-lit computer screens to reduce the glare. A gray and black diamond pattern carpet covered the floors. Two rows of computers sat side by side on identical wooden desks occupied by people furiously typing.

Terra washed her hands together. She felt out of place and didn't know where to stand. Bumped and pushed a few times until she found herself in the corner. She couldn't take her eyes off the screen. Her heartbeat was so fast it threatened to jump from her chest. A set of familiar arms wrapped around her from behind as Terra breathed in Devan's scent. Ready to face the future.

Sofia
11:33 pm

Sofia found her boys sitting on a shabby black leather couch at the back of the Control Center.

"Mom, where have you been? We were worried about you." Rob's voice quivered.

She hugged her boys close, grabbing each of their hands. The countdown clock showed two minutes left when James joined them on the couch. There was nothing they could do but sit and watch the seconds tick down. At least they were together, no matter what happened.

The electrical storm had grown. Fireballs screamed; debris blasted upward before falling to earth, destroying everything below.

The screens went dark seconds before the lights went out.

Thank you for reading Edge of Existence.
I would like to gift you with the first two chapters of Hollow Edge.

Hollow Edge

SNEAK PEAK AT HOLLOW EDGE

Prologue
June 27ᵗʰ, 2049

When the lights flickered back on, Sofia pinched herself to make sure she was still alive. She felt her husband, James Cutter, the President of the United States, squeeze her shoulder. With difficulty she raised her head, her eyes searched then lasered on to her boys; the rise and fall of their chests proof they were safe. Sofia pressed her palm against her bullet wound, relishing the pain because it meant they had survived. The bunker had withstood the blast—but now what?

As predicted, an asteroid, code-named Attila, hit Earth. It was an astrological disaster, not a political one, that almost wiped most life forms from existence. James immediately resumed his duties, rising to speak with the Secretary of Defense despite wobbly legs. Sofia knew she should do something as First Lady to comfort those surrounding her, but she didn't have the strength to move.

She looked around the command center wondering how long they would have to remain there, two thousand feet below the Earth's surface. She breathed deeply, trying not to dwell on the reality of the situation and its effects above ground.

The Cheyenne Mountain Complex, designed in the 1960s to house the government in case of a nuclear war, was located just outside Colorado Springs, Colorado. Deep underground, it spanned just under five acres. She wondered how many people were alive in the other shelters or if anyone survived outside this self-sustaining city. The complex was built to withstand the horrors like the ones that had just obliterated civilization.

NASA's Planetary Defense Coordination Office tracked Attila long before impact. Slowly the governments of Earth's major nations had stockpiled weapons, gathered seeds, collected irreplaceable art, and prepared for the unthinkable. Sofia and her family as well as the other VIPs moved into primary warning centers. The VIPS included top government officials, doctors, engineers, and specialists of every kind. People that would be useful in helping society to rebuild while working with the materials they had stockpiled. VIPS, but not their families. Some of them were taken against their will, wanting to stay with their families instead. The government didn't share the news with the public until the last minute, not wanting to start a panic, but word eventually leaked out.

The TV screens were nothing but static. Like it was scripted, everyone in the control center hurried back to their tasks trying to contact the outside world or what remained of it. How could they go back to work when everything had just changed? How could they function knowing their families were left outside?

The experts predicted that the planet would be in rough shape. They expected the asteroid would land in the Atlantic Ocean causing massive tidal waves and tsunamis that would eradicate the North American east coast. Dust from the impact would block out the sun killing most life on Earth and push the planet into a deep freeze after smaller fireballs set the planet on fire. They had already seen the damage one fireball could do when half of Colorado Springs disappeared.

Earlier, those trying to approach the fence had been shot at, not stopping until several people had been killed. Not even stopping then, but the fence had held. Both soldiers and civilians had died in the skirmish. Had Sofia done the right thing when she showed mercy and snuck civilians into the bunker? When she saw people suffering, how could she not help? They could share the space.

Already she had heard rumblings that the more senior of the VIPs weren't happy. They were asking for the establishment of a Commission and a fence to divide them from the subordinates. Looking around her at the hustle of those in duty mode, trained to do their jobs above all else, made her wonder if her rebellious act of kindness would doom them all. Only time would tell.

Chapter One
April 22, 2167

Sparks flew around my head while the monotonous popping and hissing of the welder drowned out everything else surrounding me. Lost in my thoughts, the acidy smell of burning metal fusing together flooded my nose, becoming all I could taste. The vaporizing steel invaded my lungs, my pores, every cell of my body. I couldn't wait until I could scrub the day away. Even then, after the regulation four-minute lukewarm—though forceful—spray of the shower, there was always some residue left behind.

"Useless," I muttered as a large drop of water gathered then dropped from the pipe mere inches away from the spot I had just fixed. Welding in the water plant was an endless job. The galvanized steel pipes sprung leak after leak as the bunker's infrastructure was old and worn. The welding torch in my right hand felt like a part of me, a metal extension of my body that I used twelve hours a day, six days a week. I loosened my grip, then stretched each finger individually to relieve the pain and stiffness.

Why couldn't I be ambidextrous?

Bundles of pipes and cables in various shapes and sizes ran along the sides and top of the walls. Once painted in brilliant colors, the years faded them until they became the same shade of dull. Knocking twice on the cold rock wall, I gave thanks the Hollows was still sustainable since the alternative was unthinkable. The lights flickered. Was there a problem with the generators? The underground whispers claim the diesel-filled lake is almost dry.

"Charlie. Hey, Charlie!"

My concentration broke and I released the trigger of the welding torch when I heard my name called. I cocked my ear toward the sound until I heard it again. Flipping up the visor on my helmet, I spun around, catching a glimpse of Callahan striding towards me. His footsteps in the cavernous room were muffled by the sound of the welder.

I raised a hand in an uncertain greeting, and he waved back uneasily. Glancing around, I checked to see if anyone from the Authority lingered nearby. My heart pounded so hard it threatened to burst from my ribcage. My hands became slick with sweat inside the thick leather gloves that were two sizes too big.

What would possess Callahan to visit me while I worked? If they discovered us on an unsanctioned break, there would be consequences, severe ones. Thunder—thank goodness, there was no one in sight. Various scenarios played in my mind as he walked towards me. What had happened that he has shown up here? Why would he take such a risk? I checked my tag—forty-five minutes before the final horn. Not that long. I shuffled my feet wondering if I should risk talking to Callahan or ask him to wait until the final horn sounded?

Against my better judgment, I turned off the welding torch, slipped off my gloves, and removed my helmet. My hair spilled out halfway down my back. Hurrying to throw it up in a ponytail, I pulled on the hat stuffed in my back pocket. I poked up all the loose strands into my cap, so my hair wasn't visible. I couldn't chance the paint wearing off.

"Whatcha doing here?" I swung down from the scaffolding, unsure whether to smile or frown. A visit with Callahan would usually put me in a better mood, but my stomach was queasy at the thought of someone noticing and reporting us.

"How did you find me?" Callahan mouthed the word "blind spot". He pointed towards a black security camera anchored to the arched cement wall, motioning for me to bend down. The feeble lighting reflected off the camera lens, creating moving patterns on the opposite wall. Its mechanical whirling and clicking noises reverberated in the room. We would only have a few seconds until the camera swung back our way.

I dropped into a crouch, creeping towards the blind spot where those watching couldn't see. Cameras observed us twenty-four hours a day, seven days a week. Those of us from the eastern part of the bunker, the laborers , or Subs as the Elites called us for subordinates, learned how to stay out of sight as much as possible. It had taken years to discover and map all the blind spots in the Hollows.

Big fat drops of water plopped down on our heads from the leaking water pipes. The overhead fluorescent light barely reached the edges of the corridors, enabling us to get lost in the dimness. I felt the cold rough rock wall against my back. A shiver ran through me as I thought of all the spiders and creepy crawlies that could easily touch my skin and get in my hair. A pitfall of living underground. I detested bugs.

"How's the welding going?"

Callahan wasn't acting like himself. He seemed fidgety. Restless, like he was about to jump out of his skin. His eyes darted from side to side, his head twisted over his shoulder, as if he waited for something to hop into the shadows with us.

"Still holding together so far," I replied with a half shrug. Experience taught me he was working up to telling me something else. Something I would not like.

"Good, that's good, right? Because we've been down here a long time, longer than we should have been?"

"Yup, they built this place for thirty days, not 118 years." I sighed as I checked the time, 5:15 pm. The workday would soon end.

I wasn't in the mood to rehash the history of the bunker with this senseless small talk. I monitored the camera. It swung back this way, but we should be safe here for now. "Is that what you came over here for, to discuss things we both already know? Why are you here? I need to get back to work. This can wait until the end of shift." I pointed to my tag.

His demeanor changed, as if by the flip of a switch. I watched as the pinched expression left his face. His head tilted to the side, and a ridiculous grin spanned from ear to ear. He rubbed his hands together then before I could react, splayed out his fingers, and ran them down my face, something he did from an early age when he discovered how much I hated being touched. Most times, I never reacted quick enough to move out of the way. If you told Callahan not to jump, it would be the first thing he did.

Callahan wore his sanitation uniform: black boots, gray baggy coveralls, covered with a bright orange vest. My uniform was green for maintenance, but otherwise the same. Callahan's clothing did nothing to take away the fact he was gorgeous, with jet-black hair, big brown eyes, light-brown skin and chiseled features. His short strands stood straight up, spiked like an old punk rocker, a type of music he tried to make popular again. On anyone else, his hairstyle would look ridiculous, but somehow it seemed perfect on him.

My security tag beeped. I slipped it from the holder on my left arm to read the message. I noticed Callahan's tag missing.

"An alert?" he asked.

"Just a reminder about tomorrow's assembly."

"As if we could forget with all the daily alerts and notifications they send."

"Hey, where's your security tag?" I fumbled around the sleeve of my uniform until I returned the thin black metal tag covered in plastic to its proper place. My fingers ran over the smooth cover, clutching it closer.

"Don't worry, I've got it." He gave me a flippant wave of his hand, then flashed another mischievous smile. He pulled his tag out from the inside pocket of his uniform, reattaching it to its proper place on his left arm. "I wouldn't get caught without it . . . know better than that, right?"

"If you say so. You are breaking Code 7A-1421 not being in your proper work area just being here."

Callahan glanced at the camera. "Never mind that. Guess, what? You'll never believe what I've found. Like never, ever, ever, ever, ever, ever!" Callahan pulled something out of his back pocket then stood with his hands behind his back. "Guess!"

"What are you? Twelve?"

"Just guess!" Callahan shifted his weight back and forth, unable to stay still.

His enthusiasm felt contagious. Despite my nervousness, I found a smile on my face without realizing how it got there. I was horrible at guessing games, but it meant a lot to him, so I tried. At each guess, he shook his head no. His eyes glinted. What had he found to make him react this way? I hadn't seen him this excited in a long time. Searching my brain for something, anything, I came up blank. I raised my arms in surrender. "Gees, I don't know."

Callahan dropped his hands to his sides. An apple floated out from behind his back, hovering just below his shoulders in front of his chest "Surprise!" Callahan made every simple act into a performance—although this time, an actual apple, made it worthy.

My jaw dropped. An apple, not just a picture of one. Rumors from the underground whispers boasted that apples grew in the restricted section of the food plant, but I never hoped to see one in my lifetime.

Callahan's twin sister, Gibson, and our friend, Reese, both worked in the food plant. They had never seen an apple either, probably because they couldn't access the restricted area. We chalked their existence up to a myth or an urban legend. But they actually existed. The shiny red color drew me towards it like a magnet. I couldn't look away. My hands trembled as I reached forward to touch it; but then I froze. Shrinking back, I dropped my hands interlacing them behind my back.

My head swung to check the camera even though I knew it couldn't have caught Callahan's performance. The other camera, though, must have recorded I wasn't working, that I was not standing where I was supposed to be. Interlinked with the computer system, someone would have added a note to my file.

"Jumping jeepers, Callahan Malone, are you crazy?" I swallowed down a gulp. "What are you doing with that, you'll get us both sent to the vault? Don't you know how long you could get locked up just for touching one of those?"

"Overreact much? Can you believe my good luck? I still can't." Callahan's eyebrow raised slightly. "Anyway, they wouldn't send me to the vault for a tiny infraction like this, right?"

"You sound so sure." I wanted to shake him. How could he be this reckless? My head whirled; another headache was forming. I rubbed my temples to ease the pain. "You know if you break any of the commission's codes what will happen… getting caught with contraband breaks Code 3A-2933. Not to mention using your abilities… in *public*. You need to stop doing stupid stuff or you will get both of us killed."

"I'm careful. The TCC won't catch me. Besides, they'd never blame you as you've never been in trouble before."

I looked around and whispered, "You'd better not get caught calling the commission that name."

"What are you saying?" he pretended innocence, then grimaced, "TCC stands for 'Totally Corrupt Commission' and that's what they are, right?"

"Don't repeat it." I swatted his arm. "I have to get back to work."

"Charlie, listen… I know what you are thinking, but I didn't use my powers to get the apple; I swear I didn't. I found it… honest." He crossed his hand over his chest.

"Well, you are using your powers now, aren't you? Holy Attila… hang on to the apple with your hand." My words rushed out faster than normal. "Callahan, you know better than to use your telekinesis. What if they caught you, and with the apple on top of that? Then it wouldn't just be the vault, would it? Do you want to get exiled?"

The vault meant incarceration, but exile was a sure death sentence. Nothing could survive outside of the bunker, in the frozen wasteland.

Callahan snatched the apple out of the air and spun it around on his index finger. "What's with you lately? You are even grumpier than usual."

"You—that's what!" I wiped my sweaty hands on my pant leg. "You are stressing me out right now. I don't want to get caught up in this. Why are we even friends? You live your life on the edge, and I know—I'm a boring rule follower. It's so… crazy. I can't breathe, I feel like I'm going to have a heart attack."

"Overreact much?" He raised an eyebrow.

I stared at the ceiling, trying to avoid the apple's allure. Steel netting covered the rocks overhead, anchored by over 115,000 rock bolts to keep pieces of rock from falling. Workers had hammered the bolts chaotically into the granite, so it looked like a crazy rock-climbing wall. Sometimes I imagined pictures in the design, shapes like stars and animals.

Callahan laughed at me throughout my tirade while polishing the apple on the sleeve of his coveralls. He'd seen me spin out-of-control plenty of times; it wasn't anything new.

"Um well... because you have enough fear for both of us, scaredy-cat," Callahan teased. His smile made him appear younger than his seventeen years. Callahan made big loops with his finger beside his head, like I was crazy.

I made a funny face at him, but Callahan's cheery mood immediately made me feel better.

Callahan sometimes had an endearing habit of saying "right" after every sentence. As if he needed confirmation on everything he said.

"Whatever." I couldn't stop my lips from quirking upwards. "Rules make life easier. I don't know why I've always liked them, but I do. I think it's because it makes everything black and white, right or wrong, truth or lie. I liked absolutes better than maybes."

"Do you want the first bite?" Callahan motioned to hand me the apple. Callahan embodied generosity: always willing to share what little he had. He didn't have a selfish bone in his body. Others would have saved the apple for themselves and savored it in private, but not him.

I wanted to grab the apple from his hand and discover what it felt like, smelled like. The apple shone so red and glossy—my eyes had never experienced that color before. I couldn't even imagine how it would taste. My mouth watered at the thought.

"I'll pass," I answered after a long deliberation with myself. No matter how much I wanted to taste the apple, I knew I would never let myself try it. It wasn't a risk I would take.

Callahan taunted me with a twisted half-smile. He ran his hand through his spiked hair before he took his first bite, his face lighting up with delight. He barely swallowed the first bite when he took another. Did it taste as good as it looked? My mouth salivated and I tore my eyes away from him. "Charlie, you have to live a little, take a chance, right?" He focused on the apple, mumbling and drooling as he took a bite. "When will you ever get an opportunity to try an apple again?"

He wasn't wrong. I might never get the opportunity again, but I just couldn't do it. Fear kept me from taking a bite. Fear stopped me from doing most everything. The thought of the consequences kept me in line. They were too severe; I took a big enough chance just sitting here while he ate the apple. It was out of character for me to do something this risky.

"Yeah..., no." I rubbed my temples as my headache pulsed. The initial low throb developed into a raging pain. The headaches began a few years ago, one every month or two, but lately, they were more frequent and intense.

"Headache again?"

I nodded. "If you didn't use your abilities, how did you get the...?" I motioned toward the apple, still too afraid to say the word.

"It fell off a cart coming back from the food plant." Callahan lit up as he explained. "It rolled into the corner without the Authority noticing. I snatched it, tossing it in with the trash because they never look in there when I'm cleaning. I couldn't believe my good luck."

Hiding contraband in with the trash became one method of moving things around from place to place without the Authority noticing.

"Hmm, sometimes, I guess you're lucky you have the worst job in the Hollows."

"Cause my job picking up everyone else's garbage is a dream, right?" He adjusted the collar on his uniform as if he were wearing a three-piece suit. "I'll trade you, sanitation for maintenance. You can get stuck with all the dirty jobs nobody else wants to do."

"Yuck, no thank you." My nose wrinkled at the thought.

"Are you positive? Not even to see the control center?" he nudged his shoulder against mine.

"Big deal. You've only gotten to see it once, it's not like it's an everyday event."

"That's still one more time than you saw it, right?" he continued in a singsong voice. "You could see more of the Hollows. I have access to move around almost everywhere."

"Not the West End. Plus, it's against the code 2A-9831 to access places you don't have clearance for."

"No, not the West End. Not yet, anyway." Callahan lowered his head. A wistful look appeared on his face. "Charlie, don't you ever wish you were an Elite? Imagine. You could eat amazing things like this all the time."

"Do you think they do? Or are they rationed like once a year?"

The juice from the apple trickled down his chin, washing the filth of the day from his face. I had to look away. He wiped the back of his hand across his mouth.

"Plus," I added, "what would be the point of wishing? You know things never change around here. Life is never so bad that it can't be worse."

"Damn Charlie, same old story, every time. Why are you so negative?" He glared at me, his jaw clenched, and a vein throbbed in his neck. "Life's not so bad... you're still alive, aren't you? Tomorrow is another day; you never know what could happen. Look at me: yesterday I had never even seen an apple and today I have tasted one. Life can change from moment to moment."

"I . . ." His tumultuous mood swings drove me crazy. "Expect nothing and nothing will disappoint you. You'll never get hurt."

"Unbelievable! You never look on the positive side of things." There was nothing left of the apple. He put the remnants in his pocket and licked his fingers before wiping his hands on his uniform. He dragged his hands through his hair as we stood in silence. His spikes bounced right back up.

After a few seconds, I reached over and tapped his arm. "I'm sorry, I wish I could be more like you, but... I don't know how. I'm emotionally backward."

"Um, maybe you choose pessimism, so you are never disappointed when you expected something good to happen and it doesn't, right?

"Whoa, that's deep. When did you get so poetic?" I tried to cajole him back to a better mood. He wouldn't stay mad at me for long; he never did. He always burned hot but cooled off quickly. How could he stay mad when he found an apple? Jumping jeepers, that might be the best thing that has ever happened to him.

I slide down the wall to sit on the rough concrete floor and Callahan plopped down beside me. "Did you ever wonder why the walls, floors, everything is gray; there is not a single drop of color in this place?" I asked. "Everything is so drab. Why can't we use color?"

"Nope," Callahan answered. "Never thought about it."

"Well, don't you think it would be better to see painted murals or pictures on the walls instead of stone and cement? Someone with artistic talent must live in the bunker. Maybe there could even be a modern-day Picasso or Monet."

"Who?"

"Don't you remember anything from our time at Voco?" I admonished him for forgetting. "Picasso and Monet, painters in the old world that painted famous pictures that hung in museums... I think there is a portrait hung in the assembly hall. The one with the bridge and water lilies—."

"They don't even give us enough to eat what makes you think they would give us paint for the walls... the TCC would never allow that."

I bumped his shoulder with mine. "I am fully convinced you never graduated from Voco."

"Guilty." A shadow passed behind his eyes.

I nodded. I shouldn't have brought up Voco. I knew Callahan hated talking about school. It had become a sore spot with him because of his dyslexia. The teachers didn't have extra time to spend with him, so he fell behind. We all tried to help him, but we didn't know how.

We sat together without speaking, content with the lack of words. Why weren't more people fluent in silence? I checked the location of the camera, estimating I had about ninety seconds before it would swing back around. I needed to get back to my post. The computer would have logged every minute it stood deserted.

Before I could leave, I felt my heartbeat pick up and I dropped down beside Callahan again. I sensed we weren't alone.